never so green

tim

johnston

never so green

farrar straus giroux
new york

I wish to heap thanks and praise upon the following people, each of whom, I hope, will know exactly what I'm talking about: Speer Morgan, Marianne Merola, Robbie Mayes, Elaine Chubb, René Paine, Jon Dorfman, Tyler Johnston, Mark Wisniewski, Mark Carroll, Rick Hills, and Sariah Dorbin.
—T.J.

A portion of this work has previously appeared in different form in *The Missouri Review.*

Copyright © 2002 by Tim Johnston
All rights reserved
Distributed in Canada by Douglas & McIntyre Ltd.
Printed in the United States of America
Designed by Barbara Grzeslo
First edition, 2002
1 3 5 7 9 10 8 6 4 2

Library of Congress Cataloging-in-Publication Data
Johnston, Tim.
  Never so green / Tim Johnston.— 1st ed.
    p. cm.
  Summary: In Iowa in the 1970s, twelve-year-old Tex overcomes his self-consciousness
about his deformed right hand to take baseball lessons from his stepfather and his
tomboy stepsister, who harbors a dark secret.
  ISBN 0-374-35509-6
  [1. Baseball—Fiction. 2. Stepfamilies—Fiction. 3. Physically handicapped—Fiction.
4. Sex role—Fiction. 5. Child sexual abuse—Fiction. 6. Iowa—Fiction.] I. Title.

PZ7.J6476 Ne 2002
[Fic]—dc21

                                                    2001051119

For Judy Johnston, Joe Johnston, and Amanda Potterfield

Inside the house lived a malevolent phantom. People said he existed, but Jem and I had never seen him.

—Harper Lee

To Kill a Mockingbird

never so green

1

It was five to three, and still Ms. Riley stood at the board, her arm a blur, churning out sentences as if she would never stop. If you'd been passing by and happened to glance in just then, you might've been impressed by her dedication, her youthful enthusiasm, the shapely flow of her hand. In the same moment you might've been struck by the stillness of her students, the most attentive collection of sixth-graders you'd ever seen, and you might've thought, *What a teacher! What kids!*

You might've thought such things, that is, if you were crazy, or at least very forgetful, for it was the last day of school and the only person watching the chalkboard in Ms. Riley's classroom was Ms. Riley herself. Her sixth-graders, without exception, were fixated on the clock above her, their hearts about to explode with impatience, their brains crying out in unison, *Stop writing, stop writing, stop writing!*

But Ms. Riley, pausing only to underscore her adverbs, wrote on—blissfully, tirelessly, mercilessly.

Finally, when she could not fit another word on the board, her writing arm came down and her watch arm came up. A steady rain of fingers stopped drumming desktops; sneakers gripped linoleum; nobody dared to breathe—except Ms. Riley, who took a breath and smashed all hope by talking. She'd been delighted, she began, simply *delighted*, to usher such a fine group of young men and women through the sixth grade. She would remember them always and wished to send them off with a little something, perhaps, to remember her by.

The students watched helplessly as she went behind her desk, knelt with a pop of pretty knees, and returned with a bulging grocery bag. Warned as fifth-graders about this day, no one was fooled by the colorful wrappings and carefully printed tags: Ms. Riley was giving them books. And not even new books, but books she'd bought at library sales and thrift stores and the garage sales of their own parents.

Yet they remained in their seats, her students, as the young teacher smiled on—as summer began to pass them by—and they dutifully tore open their gifts.

At his desk in the second row, Tex Donleavy, known to read books in his own free time, unwrapped a dog-eared paperback and turned it over. It was a novel called *Lord of the Flies*, by William Golding. Tex noticed other kids glancing at first pages and did the same. A batch of familiar blue ink greeted him:

To Davy Donleavy, a very special boy with a very bright future. I will never forget our wonderful conversations! With true affection, Ms. Riley

4

Tex cringed and closed the book and didn't look up. He couldn't bear to see her smiling at him just then. He felt sorry and embarrassed and angry all at once, because he wanted to keep the book but not the inscription, and he knew how lousy it was going to feel to rip it out, but what could he do? He didn't want to be reminded of the way he used to have "wonderful conversations" with Ms. Riley every chance he got, or how badly he'd once craved her "true affection." He didn't want to be reminded of the way he used to feel about Ms. Riley because he *didn't feel that way* about Ms. Riley anymore. There was somebody else, now.

At last, she opened her door, and students poured through it like water. Tex didn't fight the current but jumped right in, and if she didn't hear his "Goodbye!" as he passed, well, at least he'd said it.

Outside, the stream of kids broke apart, and Tex was left to cross the playground by himself. The rain had let up and the sun was out, raising wisps of steam from the grass. It was summer 1974, and his days at William Taft Elementary were over.

He opened his book, careful to avoid the inscription, and began to read as he walked. It was pretty good. A plane had crashed; kids much luckier than grownups were washing ashore like debris. He was so caught up in the story he didn't notice the sound of footsteps behind him, matching his pace. Then he did notice, and he slowed down. The footsteps slowed down, too. *A beating*, he thought, *on the last day of school, a fond farewell to Donleavy . . .*

He stopped, wheeled around to face his stalker, but found

only Melanie Bloom—a nice, shy, freckled girl who just that spring had undergone the promise of her name. The effect had been so dramatic that female classmates now shunned her and boys who'd previously refused to target the back of her neck with a spitwad spent all recess plotting to get themselves shoved into her.

Melanie Bloom smiled at him. "What'd you get?"

He aimed his gaze to the left, well away from her chest. "Get?" he said.

She pointed to his book.

"Oh." He showed her the cover.

"What's it about?"

He shrugged and attempted to sum up events so far. She showed him hers. "I got *Rebecca of Sunnybrook Farm*, but I've already read it. Twice." She smiled again, and he noticed her dimples.

"Must be good," he said, and walked on. Nature had cursed Melanie Bloom, and for that he liked her. But school was over, and he didn't see much point in making friends now, least of all with a girl like Melanie Bloom.

Regardless, she stuck with him. "We're practically neighbors, you know."

"We are?" They were walking toward the far corner of the school lot, where a kind of infield had been stomped permanently into the earth. Rain had turned base paths to mud, but this, Tex realized too late, was no deterrent, and a moment later a dozen boys stopped playing and turned, as one, to watch him and Melanie pass by. Eyes squinted in the shade of visors. Mitts hung slack at the ends of arms. The boys were using, Tex saw, books for bases.

Melanie talked on, a little breathlessly. "You don't say much in school, but Ms. Riley says you're pretty smart, just shy. She says that hand makes you, you know. Sensitive. But I don't mind. You don't have to keep it in your pocket."

He turned to glare at her, to give her a good sizing up; why would she pick now, of all times, to talk to him?

Unless, he suddenly thought, they'd put her up to it.

But even as he thought this, Joey Dunsmore, the outsize thug who'd flunked the sixth grade last year for the express purpose, Tex was certain, of continuing to torture him, hollered from home plate, "Hey, Melon-nee!" Tex saw her turn red and knew she was not part of the plot. He despised Joey Dunsmore—he'd have given a year's allowance to see the kid get creamed by a snowplow—but all Tex could think just then was, *Thank you, Turdbrain, for picking her and not me.*

"Hey, *Daaavy!*" Dunsmore called. "You gonna get some with that hand a yours or what?"

"Ignore them," Melanie advised.

Tex picked up the pace. "*You* ignore them," he said. "And as for *Ms.* Riley, next time you see her, tell her she doesn't know crap about anything, the ugly old bag."

Melanie stopped, and Tex marched on. When she spoke, he could hear the wobble in her throat. "Seems Ms. Riley was only half-right," she said. "You're sensitive, all right, but you're about the stupidest little creep I ever saw!"

Tex reached his backyard at ramming speed, took note of the two cars in the driveway—his father's white, year-old Thunderbird, and the beat-up, lipstick-red Mustang that always made his heart jump—before he burst through the door and crashed into a pile of luggage. The luggage was going, not coming, he concluded, and he leaped to his feet and hit the stairs, swimming pools and souvenir shops and air-conditioned hotel rooms in his mind.

He stopped when he reached his father's bedroom, and stood still. A muted ransacking was under way in the closet. He heard the thunk of tossed shoes, the jangle of wire hangers—and laughter, low and female and thrilling.

In a moment his father emerged, a strange smile on his face, his hair all out of order. His father was not famous for his sense of horseplay, and seeing him this way, dressed like an attorney but grinning like a doofus, caused two distinct pangs in Tex's heart: one for his father goofing off without him, one for him doing it with *her*, in the closet.

Jacob caught sight of his son and composed himself. "There's the graduate," he announced, tending to his hair. The knot of his tie was still tight, Tex observed, which meant he'd come straight from work and had yet to pour himself his Friday whiskey.

Tex shrugged.

"No need to be modest," Jacob said. "I'm very proud. Now." He cleared his throat and invited Tex to take a seat beside him on the edge of the bed. Tex did so, knowing that nothing good ever came out of taking a seat on the edge of his father's bed. Inside the closet, the rummaging resumed.

"Son," Jacob began, "something a little unexpected has come up."

Tex understood at once: *they* were going, he was not. "Where you going?" he asked.

Jacob adjusted his glasses. "Well, I—that is, Linda and I—have arranged for a brief vacation in the Virgin Islands. Neither of us has ever been, and it seemed an opportune time to—"

"*Islands?*" Tex said. "For how long?"

"Just a week."

"A whole week?"

"Tex, I haven't had a vacation in I don't know how long, and I've got that trial coming up, and I know this is sudden, but to tell you the truth I was counting on you being a little more charitable about it, since some folks don't get three months' vacation."

"Yeah, but—"

"I found it!" They both turned, and Linda Volesky, a metallic tennis racket in her grip, sprang from the closet. She wore cutoff jeans and a man's dress shirt knotted above the navel. She was twenty-six: exactly fourteen years older than Tex and fourteen years younger than Jacob. She flashed Tex a smile that made him want to kiss her bare feet. "Hey, handsome," she said.

"Hey," Tex said.

She gave the racket a spin—it was a Wilson T2000, the Jimmy Connors model—and crouched, bracing for a serve the likes of which she'd never see from Tex's father. She pounced on the invisible serve, backhanded it down the line, charged the net, and volleyed for the point. Tex watched all this closely, wondering if the absence of a bra made her a "women's libber." Women's liberation, Ms. Riley said, was a movement that meant to change the way society looked at women.

When Linda was finished, Tex and Jacob just sat there, staring. Finally, Tex had to know: "Why *Virgin* Islands?"

She said, "Honey, you got me!" and bounded from the room, the scent of Juicy Fruit in her wake.

As Tex packed, Jacob explained that Tex's mother and her husband were expecting him, but that as soon as he and Linda returned, Tex would be free to resume his normal schedule of every other weekend at his mother's.

Tex had seen his mother's new husband once, two months earlier, when he wasn't her husband yet. Tex had shuffled into her kitchen on a Saturday morning and found him sitting there drinking coffee and smoking a cigar. He was a big man with a big grin that didn't fade in the least when Tex declined to shake his hand. He was Farley Dickerson, the baseball coach at Jefferson High, he said, as if this explained his presence in his mother's kitchen. Tex's mother herself was head librarian. He and the coach passed another stiff minute before his mother finally appeared, red-faced and cordial. She made introductions, then saw her guest to the door. A month or so later, librarian and coach flew to Las Vegas for the weekend, and came back married. Tex still couldn't believe it. What he remembered most about Farley Dickerson was the stink of that cigar, and the toes of his cowboy boots, which seemed as long and pointed as spears.

Farley had since moved in with his mother, and brought his kids with him, though Tex had yet to meet those creatures. He pictured chubby girls with fierce plastic jump ropes, loud-mouthed boys with baseball bats.

"Take me with you!" he now begged his father.

Jacob squeezed his shoulder. "Son, you wouldn't have any fun whatsoever."

A few minutes later, seeing them off, Linda bent to plant a wet kiss near Tex's mouth. It left a print his father advised him, as he drove, to remove before they arrived at his mother's. Tex obliged him in stony silence.

Jacob drove fast but spoke at his usual methodical pace, as if nothing out of the ordinary were under way, as if he had nothing better to talk about, Tex thought, than the boring fates of his boring clients. They slowed down going through Big River, but not much, and Tex watched in vain for a police car.

"Can't we at least go to the Route 61?" he tried when they were back on the highway. "It's Sundae Friday!" Sometimes Linda would offer a cherry to Tex's lips on a spoon still warm from her mouth.

"I know, Tex," Jacob said, "but we're running late. I'm sorry."

A few miles later they swung into the drive, and Jacob brought the T-bird to a halt behind an unfamiliar, unwashed, reddish-colored VW minibus. He frowned, briefly, then gave Tex a smile. "Okay?"

Tex shoved open the door.

Jacob extracted Tex's bike, then his Samsonite bag, from the trunk. Tex let the bag keel over on the concrete.

"Hey now," Jacob said. He slipped a twenty out of his wallet. Tex hesitated, then grabbed the bill and stuffed it in his pocket, careful not to crush the small photograph already down there.

"So long, son," Jacob said, attempting to hug him. "We'll send postcards."

As the T-bird disappeared around a corner, Tex pulled out the tiny, photo-booth-size black-and-white picture. On the nights Linda stayed over, Tex would crouch in the hall closet as long as it took, his eye to the narrow crack, waiting for a glimpse of her careless nude rounds between his father's room and the bathroom across the hall. The glimpses left him dizzy, tearful, oddly despising his father, and wildly unsleepy. With the end of the school year he'd been anticipating one long summer night of crouching and waiting and glimpsing—and now all he had was this picture, small as a movie ticket and not even in color, of her face.

He stared at it and she stared back, a slight curl to her lips, her eyes silvery and clever, as if she were dying to tell him something that would turn his face bright red.

Caroline "Dickerson" took the number two pencil from her teeth and beamed at her son. "Hey, baby!" It was her nature to be delighted to see anyone at her door (Tex knew just how she'd greet all visitors to her library, swamping each one in that great big Texas smile), but he could tell she'd marshaled extra cheer just for him, just for today, as if she meant to stop his dark mood at the door. She gave him a big kiss, covering the ghost of Linda's kiss with one that smelled of grapes. His father had his Friday whiskey; his mother, her Friday wine.

"How was your last day of school?" she asked.

"Fine. How was yours?" Inside the house the familiar scent

of baked beans fought for its life against the stench of cheap cigars.

"Wonderful," she said. "I've already started a new story." She briefly elevated the Samsonite, then dropped it with a grunt. "Good grief! Did you stop at the quarry?"

"Just some books, Ma."

"Feels like the whole library."

Tex lugged the suitcase to his bedroom and stood at the window. From there he could scan the long drain of the landscape, down the hill and through the uprights of twin pines, over the edge of Archibald Creek—a minor vein feeding the Mississippi. Near the water he saw two figures, one large, one small, tossing a baseball.

Something behind him yawned and he turned to find a crib in the corner of his room. Inside the crib was a kid. A little one. Tex didn't know much about babies, but the exhausted sprawl of this one made him think he'd walked in on the single lull in a long day of locomotion and noise.

Back in the kitchen, his mother set down her pencil and stood to serve him pork and beans. "I made something in case you're hungry," she said.

"I'm not."

"Okay." She scooped his plateful back into the pot, then surprised him by pouring more wine into her coffee mug. He didn't suppose she believed she was fooling anybody with the mug, except maybe herself a little, and he didn't want to think about that. He watched her make a few corrections in her notebook.

"There's a baby in my room," he said.

"That's your little stepsister, Tex. Willa May. I couldn't get her to sleep all afternoon. Now she'll be up all night."

"She smells."

"She smells like a baby."

"Can't you put her someplace else?"

"Yes, we can. It's just, since you weren't here—"

"I'm here now."

"I see that, Tex. We'll figure something else out, okay?" She rose and went to the refrigerator. "Are you thirsty?"

"Willa May," he scoffed. "Sounds like a baseball player." Inside the fridge was a mother lode of Coca-Cola, but all Tex saw looking at so many cans was days and days without Linda. Caroline pried open a can and handed it over, and as Tex took his first swig of the summer, Farley Dickerson, bare-bellied and sweating, burst through the screen door. He grinned his big grin and reached as if to shake hands, then turned the gesture into a fake jab to Tex's ribs. "Howya been, Texaco?"

When Farley Dickerson said "Texaco," Tex heard oil rigs and longhorns. He had to wonder if it was by accident or design that his mother had married the human opposite of his father.

Farley produced a cigar and eyeballed Tex's Coke. "Got any other cold beverage, baby?"

"You know where it is," Caroline said.

Farley winked at Tex. "I guess I do."

Tex turned to the window and took another swallow of Coke. He wanted to be alone with Linda's picture.

The door banged again and in walked a skinny kid wearing baggy cutoffs and a bright red baseball cap. Seeing Tex, the kid seemed to change slightly, as if some stiff, unhappy ghost had entered his skin. He slapped a mitt against a gangly leg. His too-big T-shirt featured a pair of faded cardinals perched on a baseball bat.

Tex slipped his right hand into his pocket, and Caroline jumped to attention. "Tex, baby. This here's Jack. Jack, this is Tex. I do believe you all are the identical same age—very nearly thirteen?"

Jack squinted green eyes. "Mine's July seventeenth."

A lie seemed prudent, but there was his mother, smiling beside him like the Cattle Queen. Tex caved in with a shrug. "September fifth."

Jack helped himself to a Coke, ripped it open with beer-drinker gusto, chugged it on his way to the door. At the threshold, he turned to stare Tex down.

"Well," he said. "You comin' or what?"

"What the hell kind of name is Tex?" Jack said, leading him toward the Archibald. Like Farley, Jack Dickerson loaded his name with a disturbing twang. He tossed a ball into his mitt as he walked. He was a lefty.

"It's a nickname," Tex said. "Got a problem with it?"

Jack shrugged sharp little shoulders. "Not if you like being nicknamed after the biggest hick state in America."

Tex considered explaining how his parents had met at the University of Texas and were married in a church near the Alamo, and how, when you got right down to it, "Tex" beat the hell out of "Davy."

"I was named after a ballplayer," Jack said. "One of the greats."

"Which one?"

"You wouldn't know him."

"Says who?"

Their eyes met, and Tex recognized a bluff in the making. Jack said, "Ever hear of Jack Robinson?"

It took Tex a moment. "You mean *Jackie* Robinson?"

Jack showed him a fist. "Make something of it?"

Tex blinked at him, unintimidated, yet sorry for whatever the kid thought he'd meant. Jack held his stare long enough for Tex to notice his eyelashes—they were longer and darker, even, than Linda's—before walking on.

A moment later, Jack halted, stooped, and pulled from the weeds near the water an adult-size mitt, a right-hander's, well worn and ripe with sweat. He dangled it before Tex.

Tex thought of Joey Dunsmore and Melanie Bloom, and hotly grabbed the mitt. "What am I supposed to do with this?"

"Catch."

"What, a disease?"

Jack snorted. "Catch, tardo. As in catch a fastball?" He held a greenish Spalding to Tex's face. "Farley tried to tell me you don't play, but I said that's crazy. It's summer and school's over, so what kind of kid's gonna be inside *reading* when he could be outside playing catch?"

Tex could just hear his mother's plea to Farley to downplay the baseball thing: "Tex is such a sensitive boy, a reader, and what with that hand and all . . ." The sun was low in the sky, yet Tex felt scorched. He silently wished disaster on his father's plane: a crash just short of the Virgin Islands, no adult survivors. Or maybe one. Female.

"It's a boring game," he said.

"That's 'cause you never tried."

"Says who?"

Jack shrugged. "Don't *look* like it, is all."

"Like what."

"Like a ballplayer."

Tex took a good long look at Jack Dickerson, his meatless arms, knees like a day-old calf's, and dropped Farley's mitt. "I'm a lefty," he said, "same as you." He held out his hand for the ball.

Jack smirked, flipped him the ball, and sauntered off to an imaginary home plate. Tex pulled his right hand from his pocket and gave Jack a view of his profile, as he'd seen pitchers do. Jack dropped into a bony squat.

"Ready, ballplayer?" Tex called.

"Watch you don't chuck it in the water," answered Jack.

Tex took a breath and, with the calm of pure hatred, let the ball fly. Jack fell back an instant before Tex heard the fat smack of contact. Jack regained his feet, and Tex came forward. Jack was chewing his lip, staring into his glove as if he held something dead there.

Tex stepped closer. "Hurt?"

Jack huffed. "Right."

Tex walked up to him, his right hand swinging free of its pocket. In the womb, Dr. Freeman once explained, Tex had managed to coil the umbilical cord around that hand ("Like you thought it was the dinner bell!" the doctor joked), so that by the time Tex was born, hand and cord had to be separated by scalpel. The result was a scarred, purple, achy little paw that neither surgery nor years of physical therapy could induce to open a can of Coke. When he was nine, inspired by a matinee he'd attended several times at the Galaxy Theater, Tex began calling it The Crawling Hand. These days, it was simply The Hand. Minutes after she met him, Linda coaxed it from his pocket in order to read his fortune. "I think it's the most beautiful, sensitive hand I've ever seen," she said, and before she was through tracing the first webby scar with her finger, Tex was in love with her.

Now he reached for Jack's mitt with The Hand, and Jack got an eyeful. "What happened there?"

"Came that way," Tex said. "How about yours?" He pulled the glove from Jack's hand and they both had a look. The flesh of the palm was white and his fingers, by comparison, seemed pink and small as baby mice.

Jack shrugged. "Big deal."

"C'mere." Tex led him to the lip of the creek and down the muddy bank. They found a slab of concrete to sit on, removed their shoes, and dipped in their feet. Jack lowered his hand between his ankles and hissed. "That's a helluva sidearm there, Tex. Your dad teach you that?"

He shook his head, recalling a shameful memory: his eighth birthday, a Junior Leaguer MacGregor mitt and Official Spalding from his father—the excitement, the struggle to get his fingers into the glove, the giving up and running off in humiliation. The MacGregor had gone into storage, but the

Spalding had been thrown against a tree until it fell to pieces. Tex had not asked for another one.

Now he dug a small flat stone from the mud, wiped it smooth, and four-skipped it upstream. "Eight's my record."

Jack nodded. Tex held the boy's glove, a Rawlings, in his hands. Stan Musial's signature had been branded into the heel.

"Try it on," Jack said.

Tex held up The Hand to remind him.

"So? Here."

"No—"

But he grabbed Tex's wrist with his wet hand and began forcing the mouth of the glove over the unwilling fingers. The leather felt stiff but warm, like the inside of something live. Jack tugged at the mitt until it chewed Tex's fingers into a knot.

"No go, Jack."

"Hold on." Jack leaned into him, and before Tex could pull away, Jack's hand was inside the mitt, wrestling with his own like an angry little monkey, plugging fingers one at a time into sockets of leather. A warm flood of embarrassment shook him: no one but Dr. Freeman and Linda Volesky had touched him there in years.

Jack gave a last tug on the mitt, and when he leaned away, Tex was wearing a baseball glove for the first time ever.

"How's it feel?"

He raised the mitt to the setting sun. It was huge and tan and stitched together with fat leather sutures. It gave off an agreeable, oily scent.

"Not bad."

"Go like this." Jack made a beak of his thumb and fingers, quacked it soundlessly.

With effort the big thumb moved toward the four leather fingers. Inside the mitt, The Hand felt torn in half.

"Now you look like a ballplayer," Jack said.

"Yeah?"

"Definitely."

Tex held up the mitt, then let it fall with a sigh. "How much of a ballplayer can a guy be with a paw like mine?"

"There's worse things to be than bum-handed, Tex." He said it as if he knew, personally, the truth of this statement, but, looking at him, Tex saw no flaw, no humiliating deformity, and he answered with scorn, "Says you."

"Says me and Mickey Mantle," Jack said, "three-time MVP with bum legs. Says me and ol' Jackie the First, for crying out loud. Try being the first black guy in the majors. Hell's bells, Tex." He gave him a nudge. "You got it easy."

"Yeah?" Tex swatted him back with the glove.

"Yeah." Jack splashed water with a flick of his toes, and Tex countered by slapping his foot in the creek, dousing them both. Jack scooped a handful into Tex's lap; Tex kicked back a small tidal wave. Jack tried to push him in, but with his good hand Tex grabbed one big sleeve and pulled them both stumbling into water.

"Don't soak my mitt!" Jack cried, searching for footing, laughing.

"Serve you right," Tex said. His feet found the familiar muck, and he stood straight, leaning into the current. A step upstream, Jack stood smiling, lashes black and matted with water, eyes green as grass. They stood there grinning at each other, sure-thing friends, safe-bet brothers, when Tex noticed Jack's T-shirt. Water had pulled the two cardinals low on his rib cage, and in their place, chest-high, unmistakable beneath the wet grip of cotton, sat two small lumps.

2

Wordlessly, sullenly, Tex joined Farley at the dinner table. It was just the two of them until, at last, Caroline returned from Jack's room and took a seat. "She's not hungry," she reported. "And she's keeping Willa May. They're in the middle of a *very* compelling game."

Tex worried that Farley wouldn't stand for it, that he'd make his daughters come to dinner, but he only shrugged and turned to watch the TV, murmuring away in the living room. "Watch, Tex," he said. "Five bucks he singles to right." The batter did.

"Gee," Tex said.

Farley licked pork-chop grease from his fingers and got up. "Know what? I'm gonna move this feast into the other room. Tex, care to join me? Cubs are making it interesting."

Tex said he'd be along, just as soon as the dishes were done. Farley said *"Ha!"* as if Tex had cracked a good one—then just stared at him. Then turned to go, shaking his head.

Tex drew the water while his mother slipped flawless, slender hands into yellow Rubbermaids. Rummaging in suds, she began to sing an old song about summer winds. In her younger days, she liked to remind him, she'd sung semiprofessionally, which always made Tex think of baseball: his mother had sung awhile in the minors but never got to belt a tune in the Big Leagues.

Usually, he loved to hear her sing—but he was not feeling very usual. He took a plate and rinsed it. "So," he said. "Ol' Jack Dickerson's a girl."

"Of course she is," Caroline said. "What did you think?" She fussed with suds a moment. "Easy mistake, though. I thought the same thing at first. What with that short hair and all."

"You could've told me," Tex said. "Somebody could've warned me."

"Why? What happened, Tex?"

"Nothing. I just didn't know. We were out goofing around like two normal kids and it just—" He took a breath. "It's damned embarrassing, is all."

"Tex." Caroline simulated a frown, then tipped back her coffee mug for the last drops. She stared into the empty mug for some time before plunging it, at last, into suds. She rinsed and handed it over. "Nothing to be embarrassed about," she said. "Plenty of girls play sports these days. It's the seventies."

Tex dried the mug and put it away. "That's not the point. I don't care about that."

From the other end of the house, through doors and walls, he heard Willa May shriek with pleasure.

"Aw, hell," Tex said. "Who gives a crap anyway."

"Young man."

He tossed the towel on the counter. "I just wish I'd known, is all."

It was the top of the ninth before Tex spoke again. Farley turned from the TV to look at him. "What did you say?"

The batter flied out to center, scoring the runner.

"Sacrifice fly," Tex repeated.

Farley stared at him. "You ever *play* baseball, son?"

Tex held up The Hand for an answer. Farley pried the tab on another beer, and Tex got up and headed for his room. As he passed the bathroom, his mother reached out to tell him, eyebrow tweezers in hand, that she'd moved Willa May into Jack's room.

"Thanks," he muttered, and shut his door behind him.

He switched on his reading lamp and saw Jack's mitt on his bed, where he'd left it. He picked it up and jammed in The Hand, pushed and pulled until all five fingers were in place. He squeezed the mitt shut despite the pain, opened it, squeezed again, recalling the cool touch of his—her—fingertips. He heard the toilet flush, waited for his mother to pass, then stepped into the glow of the hallway night-light. Jack's room, formerly the storage room, was next to his, their beds separated by some plaster and paint. No light seeped from under her door, but he could hear the faint insect voices of a transistor radio: the Cubs had blown it.

"Bonehead freakin' Cubbies," Farley mumbled from the living room.

Tex set the mitt in front of her door and returned to his

room. He unpacked *Lord of the Flies* but didn't seem able to focus on the words. He blinked, squinted, and held the book an inch from his face before tossing it aside, finally, and undressing.

A moment later, lying in the dark, listening to the distant belch of frogs, he remembered that at first daylight his mother would grab his clothes and stuff them in the Maytag, gutting all pockets as a matter of course. He flicked on the lamp and found his pants, rooted out Linda's picture, propped himself against the headboard. He held the picture with The Hand and could almost smell the lilac scent of her shampoo. She gazed back with lips on the verge of speaking, saying the words *beautiful, sensitive . . .*

He switched off the lamp and with his good hand reached under the sheets. He shut his eyes and imagined white sand and blue sea, a deserted beach, a woman staggering now out of the surf, limbs netted in seaweed and the remnants of a man's white dress shirt. Using a Wilson T2000 for support, the woman gains dry land, kneels, and weeps for the loss of her elderly traveling companion. Some fortune-teller she turned out to be! she thinks. In another moment she forces herself to stand. "Must find a phone," she tells herself, "must contact Tex . . ." She strips seaweed from her thighs, white cloth from her arms, and begins a brisk march inland. She even whistles a little, practices her overhand volley as she makes her bare, bouncy, sea-glazed way to—

A door clicked shut and Tex froze. Through the wall he heard Jack's bed squeak, and jerked his hand from beneath the sheet.

He sat up, his heart pounding, and strained to hear.

Nothing but frogs.

He waited for his heart to calm down, then tried to get back to his fantasy, to pick up where he'd left off, but Jack Dickerson got in the way. The memory of her standing in the Archibald, T-shirt clinging, jumped in where Linda had been, and Tex burned with fresh embarrassment. What a moron he was! How could he not have known?

The frogs answered with the steady pulse of their throats, and before long Tex was so close to sleep he almost didn't hear the whispers and squeaks, and when he did hear them he took them for the shivering of leaves in a storm front, the creak of rusty links on the swing set next door. Gradually, he revived enough to understand that the noises were coming from the other side of the wall.

He scooted over, pressed his ear to the paint, and listened to patchy, unintelligible whispering. Then, abruptly, the bed creaked, footsteps crossed the floor, and her door opened. Tex waited to hear her open and close the bathroom door across the hall. Instead, as if she'd paused a long time at the threshold, then changed her mind, her door clicked shut, and she was suddenly back in bed, settling in, sighing.

Talking to the baby? he wondered. Or had his mother been in there, pestering them with sleepy, wine-sweet mothering?

In a moment a soft swatting sound came through the wall, as if someone was receiving a slow, deliberate spanking— and suddenly Tex got it. He crept to his door, opened it, and peered around the jamb. Her mitt was gone.

Doofus! he thought, returning to bed. *She's playing catch!*

He pictured her lying on the other side of the wall, tossing the ball straight up, watching it hang for a moment moon-blue against the ceiling, fielding it with the Rawlings—and waited for his heart to stop pounding.

He woke up late the next day, damp with sweat. He reached to scratch his thigh and found something stuck there: Linda's picture, limp as a decal. He peeled it off and looked her over. She seemed slightly faded, eyes more white than silver, her lips a sickly gray. A lousy picture of her, really.

He stuck the photograph between the pages of his book, shoved the book under his bed, and went to see what the first full day of summer would bring.

"Okay, Jack, bring it home, now." Farley pounded his mitt and crouched, shirtless, where Jack, awaiting Tex's pitch, had crouched the day before. Jack stood where Tex had stood.

Tex kept his distance as she checked a phantom base runner, wound up, and pitched the ball.

"Little high and wide, Jackie, but good zip. Good hum." Farley tossed it back. "Now gimme a strike, darlin'."

Jack muttered something to the grass, took a breath, and pitched again. Farley sprang to his right and with the very lips of his mitt saved the ball from the Archibald.

"That's all right, Jack. That's okay." He trotted forward, a pale man of Jell-O. "Had some good heat on the ball. Just gotta control it, is all. Focus it." He held out the ball, dropped it in his daughter's mitt. "Okay?"

"Sure." Jack kicked, beheading a dandelion.

"Okay, then." He gave her a pat to the back pockets, man to man.

"Hey, Tex," Farley said. "Finally decide to join the living?"

Tex squinted at the man's gut.

"Well, grab a mitt, son, and we'll triangle!"

Tex looked around, turned a full 360, made a face like, *Damn, who ran off with my glove?*

Farley elbowed Jack. "The boy's got a sense of humor."

Jack shot Tex an icy glance. "He's a riot, all right."

"No glove, huh? Well now, Jack, what are we gonna—"

"In the weeds," she said. "Look in the damn weeds."

Farley turned a frown on his daughter, but was all smiles looking back at Tex. "Go on," he said.

Tex stepped toward the creek and came upon a brown object burrowed in the growth. One red "R" stared like an eye, and he felt a jolt to his chest. He collected the glove from the grass.

"It's a Rawlings," Farley said. "Jack picked it out."

Jack ground the ball into her mitt.

"Go ahead," Farley said. "Try it on."

Tex pulled The Hand from his pocket and sank it into the glove.

"Well?" Farley said.

It felt like a cast, like a solid shell; it made Tex wonder how Jack and the boys of William Taft Elementary, even with their strong normal hands, managed to put the things to any practical use. But it was a real glove, a beauty even Dunsmore would admire, and Tex could hardly believe the thrill it gave him.

"Feels great," he said.

28

"Honest?" Farley said.

Tex shrugged. "Bit stiff, is all."

"Course it is! New gloves are always stiff. As we used to say in the minors, new gloves are like shoes and women." He glanced at his daughter. "Pardon the expression, darlin', but they gotta be broken in. Now get on back a ways, Tex. Jack, you stay put, and I'll—"

"Far-leee!" came Caroline's clear, tuneful voice.

"*What?*" he barked back, and Jack turned to Tex, met his eyes for the first time since they stood in the water the day before. Tex resumed his fascination with the Rawlings.

"Telephone!" Caroline called.

Farley took a few steps toward the house, then about-faced. "Get started breaking in that mitt, Tex. I'll be right back."

The moment he was gone, Jack seemed to take her first real breaths of the day. She looked Tex in the eyes and smiled. "Your dad that retarded?"

"Worse," Tex confessed. "All he does is read."

"He remarried, too?"

"Naw. Just dating some bimbo about half his age." Tex impressed himself with that word, *bimbo*, and Jack gave a laugh, but he instantly wanted to take it back. Linda Volesky was no bimbo.

"How's that glove really feel?" Jack asked.

"Ever slam your fingers in a car door?"

"Here." She pulled off her mitt. "Use mine for a while, and I'll use yours, just to break it in, since I'm pretty good at breaking in gloves. Deal?"

"Just temporary?"

"Just temporary."

Tex yanked off the Rawlings and they exchanged. Her mitt was still warm, a little damp, blissfully soft by comparison. He gave it a punch with his good hand. "Was he really in the minors, your dad?"

"Five years at third base. 'The Infield Wall,' they called him."

"Because he's so—"

Jack shrugged. "Mostly for his glove work."

"Ever see him play?"

"Real ball? Naw. I was too young. But back in Phoenix he'd play cards with these guys and they'd tell me stories, you know, about how good he'd been. Ballplayer stuff."

Tex nodded, trying to imagine his own father at a table of men tossing cards and telling stories. It wasn't easy.

"Farley saw you pitch that ball yesterday," Jack said. "Told me this morning, 'We got to get that boy a glove!'" She smiled, but not as though this were her happiest recollection. She looked repeatedly toward the house, and in that nervous glance Tex thought he read a simple, grim truth: Jack had heart, all the heart of a true ballplayer, but she would never blast one high and deep over the ivy at Wrigley Field.

That night after dinner, while Jack gave her little sister a bath, Farley had Tex follow him out into the purple dusk. Tex still wore Jack's mitt and it was weird, he found, to use it in a game of catch with Farley. Each time he raised the mitt he felt Jack's absence acutely.

"You got a good arm, Tex." Farley returned the ball. "With practice you could be a helluva pitcher."

Despite his new, somewhat amazing appetite for Farley's praise, Tex couldn't help thinking how it would sting Jack if she could hear it. Finally, in a fit of guilt and anger, he aimed a cream puff at his stepfather's feet.

"Bush league, Tex!" Farley shot back the ball and squatted. "C'mon, now. Show me your fastball, you sidearming, south-paw son of a librarian. Lemme see it."

What *did* the librarian see in this guy? Tex brooded. He had the sudden urge to throw the ball as hard as he could at a singular target—that lump, that bull's-eye between the man's thighs. He felt lethally accurate. He gave it his best shot.

But Farley's glove work was good. "Whoo-whee!" he cried. He came trotting over. "You ever think about Little League, son?"

"What about it?"

Farley scratched his jaw. He tried again: "Have you ever thought about playing Little League baseball?"

Tex looked away. Of course he'd thought about it. He'd *always* thought about it. "Yeah, but . . ."

"Yeah but what?"

"I mean, it's too late. Isn't it?" He meant: too late for him, in life, to start playing ball.

But Farley heard something else. "With all this rain," he said, "the board voted to push the season back two weeks so fields can get planted. Soybeans first, baseball second. You got till Monday to sign up."

Tex shrugged, his insides twisting. He never knew how much he envied Dunsmore and the other boys at Taft with their full-size gloves until he'd been given one of his own—a Rawlings with a finger hole and an Edge-U-Cated heel and the endorsement of Reggie Jackson. But the best glove in the world wouldn't hide The Hand forever, he knew, and he shuddered at the thought of going to bat, of running bases, of exposing the thing to fans and players.

"I don't know," he said at last. "My dad might not let me."

"Not let you? Why the heck—" Farley looked away. "I don't know much, Tex, but I know you got an arm, and if you were my son I'd sure as hell—" He took a breath. "But you're not, so I guess that's that."

They both stared off at the moon, rising deformed and splotchy in the sky.

"I never played," Tex said. "And those other guys have been playing forever, and I'm just not, you know. Like them."

Farley smiled patiently down at him. "Jack's got the same line. Doesn't want to play softball in junior high because it's a buncha girls, can't play hardball because she is one. That kid hasn't quite caught on that she can be both, a girl and a ballplayer."

Tex stared at Jack's mitt, confused and humiliated by the comparison.

"Hell's bells, Tex. All I'm trying to say is you can still be smart, you can still read books, you can still have that funny little hand—"

Hatred flared in his chest but blew out quickly: Farley was fat and loud and rough, but not exactly mean. He just seemed to say whatever he felt in the fewest possible words.

"Tell you what," Farley said, "when I was growing up in Phoenix? Couldn't swing a dead cat without hitting a smart-ass with a fat-boy joke." His eyes went wide. " 'Somebody call

Captain Ahab! I just spotted Moby Dickerson!' 'That you, Dickerson, or am I seeing double?' " He laughed and took the ball from Tex's hand. "Then I went to junior high, and on the first day of school the coach walks up and asks me do I play football. I lie and say sure I do, and he puts me in at center so I can snap to a kid half my size, give him plenty of time to throw his bonehead interceptions. The smart-asses let up, for the most part, but I still *felt* fat. Still felt like somebody nobody else would ever want to be."

He squinted, and Tex followed his gaze to the Archibald.

"Then that spring," Farley continued, "for gym class, Coach dragged out the mitts and bats and softballs. He picked teams, looked us over, and barked out the lineup. Maybe he didn't think about it much, maybe it was just, you know, chance, but when he got to me he spoke three words I'll never forget, Tex."

Tex was betting on a fat-boy joke.

"Dickerson bats cleanup." Farley eyed him. "You know what cleanup is?"

"Fourth batter."

"Exactly. This was slow-pitch freakin' softball, mind you, but in my first at bat I air-mailed a three-run homer over the center fielder's head and through, I mean clean through, the frosted-glass window of the girls' locker room." He flexed an eyebrow for emphasis: *girls'* locker room—as if he'd been aiming for it. "Nobody ever called me Moby Dickerson so long as I was swinging a bat, and I swung my way through college and into the minors before the ol' big-league train ran out of steam."

He led Tex from the Archibald toward the house. "But the point is, Tex, you gotta find your own natural game in life. Whether it's defending crooks like your dad or writing stories like your mom's trying to do, or coaching ball like me. The trick is finding that one particular game. Then, once you do, nobody worth a damn will ever give you grief again, 'cause they'll see it in your eyes. They'll see what everyone wants to be one time or another in their short damn lives." He held out the Spalding; Tex opened Jack's mitt and Farley dropped the ball in. "Which is a ballplayer."

3

Caroline had already layered his clothes into the Samsonite, leaving Tex to gather his books. But after pulling out *Lord of the Flies* and trying to shake it free of dust, he shoved the entire pile back under the bed, snapped shut the suitcase, and went to watch the Cardinals with Jack and Farley. In the bottom of the seventh, as Bob Gibson hung on to his no-hitter, Caroline walked in and announced, butler style, that Jacob had arrived.

Farley gave Tex a swat goodbye, and Jack saw him to the door. Staring at her own bare toes, she said, "See you in a coupla weeks, I guess."

"I guess." It occurred to Tex that, with telephones and bicycles, they could easily manage visits in the meantime, or halfway meetings in Big River, but he was not about to suggest it. At the door, saying goodbye, Jack seemed more like a girl than ever, and Tex was actually grateful for the sight of his father trying to load his bike into the trunk, something to watch.

"So," Jack said, "how come you live with him, anyway?"

"My dad?" Tex watched his father, somewhat stumped. After the divorce he'd simply gone with Jacob to live in the big Victorian he'd bought close to Tex's school, which for Tex meant no more rides on that craft of torment, the public school bus. As far as Tex knew, there'd been no disputes about this arrangement, though both his parents had gone blue in the face making sure he knew they loved and wanted him equally.

"Seemed like the thing to do," he said at last. "How about you?"

Jack looked away. "No choice."

Tex stared at her, knowing she meant one of two things, but not knowing which was worse: a mother who didn't want you or no mother at all. "She isn't," he began. "I mean your mom's not . . ."

Jack shrugged. "I'm pretty much over it."

Tex shook his head, dumbfounded—a dead mother!

Yet he was less bothered by the information itself, he discovered, than by the fact that he hadn't been told. What else would he have to find out about Jack by stumbling like a doofus into it?

"Here," he said after a moment.

She took his glove. "What am I supposed to do with this?"

"Keep working on it."

"Wait, I'll get mine."

"No, don't."

Jack squinted at him, then at the floor, and Tex rushed to

explain. "I mean, hell's bells, Jack. What am I gonna do with a glove at *my* place?"

She watched Jacob for a moment, and nodded. "Take this, at least." She held out the Spalding. "Real pitchers are never without."

On the drive home, Jacob and Tex gave clipped, obligatory summations of their time apart: the islands were beautiful but entirely boring, Tex was advised, while Jacob learned that his son's new relatives were weird but tolerable. Then they fell silent. One watched the road and the other studied the red stitches of a baseball. At last they pulled into the drive, and Tex felt his heart jump at the sight of Linda's Mustang. But it wasn't the same jump as before, he realized—it wasn't just the thrill of knowing she was here; it was the shock of realizing he hadn't thought about her for days.

And with that shock came a second one: her picture. He'd left it behind. He recalled shaking the book for dust and guessed that his sweat had altered the emulsion, turned it gluey, so that anyone trying to pull the picture loose would come away with a page of book. He imagined Jack snooping around his room, finding the book and sitting on his mattress, picking at the picture with chewed dirty nails, wondering who it could be, giving up and going to bed, still wondering as she tossed a Spalding and caught it with his Rawlings.

Jacob parked the car, got out, bent to watch Tex a moment, then got back in.

"What's on your mind, son?"

"Jackie," he said. "Robinson."

"One of the greats." Jacob reached for the Spalding. Without it, even Tex's good hand felt useless. Jacob gave the ball a look and flipped it back.

"He was black," Tex said.

"I know. I had the good fortune to see him play."

Tex was stunned, as much by the idea of his father's seeing Jackie Robinson play as by his calling it his "good fortune."

"When was that?" he asked, warily.

"That first year in the majors. Nineteen forty-seven. I was spending a week with my grandparents in New York. Your great-grandfather John liked to tell people the only thing he loved more than the Bums was your great-grandmother, but I think she knew better." Jacob smiled. Tex waited.

"Anyway," Jacob said. "Grandpa John had tickets to a three-game series with Philadelphia, and for three days we took the trolley to Ebbets Field and heard those Phillies give Jackie Robinson the worst verbal lashing you could imagine, I mean vicious, relentless slander every time he stepped to the plate or took the field. But Robinson . . ." Jacob shook his head. "He just stood in the box and got his hits. Stole his bases. The Philly dugout never let up and Robinson never responded, and I remember being furious—at Robinson—for that. Why in God's name would a man take all that abuse?"

Jacob looked at Tex for a moment as though he expected an answer, though Tex knew he didn't. To Tex, it seemed as though his father had been keeping a secret all these years: he was a baseball fan.

"Then, on the last day of the series," Jacob continued, "after some five or six more innings of outrageous insults from the Phils, one of the Dodgers, I believe it was Ed Stanky, jumped from the dugout and yelled to the Philly bench so all of Ebbets Field could hear, 'Listen, you yellow-bellied bastards, why don't you yell at somebody who can answer back?' I was more confused than ever by Robinson's silence, and Grandpa John, no great student of human behavior, wasn't much help."

Jacob paused, and Tex wondered where he was going with this. It was one of his father's most annoying habits to reach ordinary points by complicated routes.

"It wasn't until a few years later," Jacob resumed, "when the league was full of African American athletes, that I read about Branch Rickey, the Dodger president, and how he'd scoured the Negro Leagues, as they were called, for a player who could hold his own and hold his tongue. Rickey wanted someone who wouldn't give the jerks and bigots the satisfaction of taking the bait—which would only incite trouble on the field and prove that players of color were bad for baseball. Rickey wanted a guy who had the guts to take it and not dish it out. Only then did I understand why Jackie Robinson kept silent those three days in Brooklyn. You see, Tex, he'd been presented with a Hobson's choice: swallow his pride and play by Rickey's rules, or don't play at all. Robinson swallowed his pride so others would get the chance to play, too. He played for Willie Mays and Hank Aaron. He played for us all, really."

Jacob reached to adjust his glasses, aging himself instantly from a boy in the bleachers at Ebbets Field to Tex's middle-aged, lawyerly father, and though Tex felt Farley had made a clearer one in a shorter time with his talk about finding that

One Particular Game, he guessed he got the point: sometimes, his father meant to alert him, it takes more guts to be less proud. It made him think again of his eighth birthday, the new MacGregor, how quickly he'd given up. Was that why his father never talked about baseball?

"I'm gonna play for Farley's Little League team," he now said.

Jacob had the poker face of a trial lawyer—no witness ever said a word he wasn't ready for—but Tex knew he'd just about knocked him out of his wing tips. "Oh?" he said.

"He's a coach, you know."

"I do know."

Tex stared at Jack's ball, waiting for his father to betray, however subtly, his opinion of the man his ex-wife had married. When he didn't, Tex asked, "Have you met him?"

"Not face to face. Is he, ah . . ." He cleared his throat. "Do you get along?"

"He's okay. He thinks I could pitch."

"In Little League."

Tex gripped the ball hard. "I've got a good arm, Dad."

"I have no doubt, Tex. I only meant . . ." He checked his watch. He adjusted the rearview mirror. "Hasn't practice begun?"

Tex explained the rain delay while his heart bounced back and forth: he didn't want to leave his father and Linda, but he felt tugged in the direction of his mother's house like a stick in a strong current.

"I'd have to spend the summer over there, probably. So I could practice with Farley. And Jack."

"Jack?"

"Jackie. Farley's daughter. She goes by Jack."

Jacob turned to observe his son. He wanted him to look up, Tex knew, to look him in the eye like a good witness, but Tex couldn't. He couldn't take his eyes off the ball.

4

Farley returned from the annual coaches' meeting like a jolly summer Santa, lugging a green equipment duffel and promising Tex and Jack that this was the season his Minnesota Twins would bring home the pennant. He'd managed, by obscure means involving beer and a full house, to secure a shortstop named Andrew Ferguson, and if Tex's pitching shaped up like he was sure it would, the Twins stood every chance of unseating the three-year-running District Champion Orioles despite a cheating S.O.B. coach and his cast of overage ringers.

Throughout Farley's speech, Jack flipped a ball in the air and caught it. When Farley finally noticed her lack of attention, he smiled, gave Tex a wink, and said, "Best news of all, Jack? I talked the board into letting you practice."

Jack faced him. "Practice?"

Farley stretched his smile. "Every Saturday, with the team. With me and Tex. Plus, I fought off three other fathers to sign you on as Official Twins Batgirl."

"But not to play." She mashed a mosquito on her thigh.

Farley shook his head to indicate his deepest frustration with Big River Little League and the small-minded world at large. "Rules are rules, darlin'."

Standing there with her hip jutting, her shoulders drawn back, and her eyes throwing hot green sparks, Jack appeared to Tex suddenly, fiercely female. "I'll practice with all those stupid no-talent boys," she told her father, "and I'll sit in the bleachers and watch Tex pitch, but I'll be damned if I'll be your Official damn Batgirl." She stormed toward the house, then, stunning Tex with the swift scissoring of her thin, pretty legs.

"Jack, darlin'," Farley tried.

"And *don't*," she said without turning, "call me darling."

Farley held Tex prisoner the rest of the afternoon with the rudiments of batting. Rightly estimating the challenge, he humiliated Tex by pulling from the green duffel a long, cloth-taped canoe paddle he called a fungo bat and a big spongy softball, and only when Tex had succeeded in fouling the ball into the Archibald did Farley produce a small Louisville Slugger and a nest of regulation Spaldings. He lobbed Tex softies from thirty feet and coached him in stance, grip, and the law of Eye on the Ball. For a long while Tex's bat happily diced up nothing but gnats. Then, suddenly, he felt the shock of connection like a wonderful cracking of a kinked-up spine, the ball shot past Farley's glove, and they both yelled out, Farley with joy and relief, Tex with joy and pain: The Hand felt plunged in boiling water. Yet he continued to connect, and

Farley chased down the Spaldings, sweating and wishing aloud that Jack would get over her snit and come back out.

Tex wished she would, too, not just to chase balls but to watch, to witness a miracle: he, Tex Donleavy, was hitting baseballs. He never wanted it to end, The Hand was numb beyond pain, but at last Farley signaled for a time out, slapped Tex on the back, and headed for Budweiser. "We'll work some more later, slugger, after it cools off."

Tex followed him into the house, repeating the word in his head. *Slugger.* He took two Cokes from the fridge, one to drink and one to hold like an icepack in The Hand, then went to find Jack. Her door was open, and, being a slugger, he walked right in.

She sat cross-legged on her bed reading *Sports Illustrated.* "What do you want?" she said without looking up.

Tex remembered the extra Coke and handed it over. She accepted without thanks and returned to her magazine, leaving him to glance around. The room was a mess, strewn clothes and magazines, a peeling poster of Lou Brock on one wall, colorful felt pennants tacked up willy-nilly. Crammed into a corner, Willa May's crib looked less like a way to keep the kid in than a way to keep Jack's room out.

"So," he said. "You're gonna practice with the team."

She shrugged. "Beats staying home all day."

On her desk, in a small gilt frame, was a faded color photograph, a foursome he didn't think he knew until he bent closer and recognized Farley, his arm around the woman beside him, forcing her skinny pale arms together as if he were not aware that she was holding a baby. The woman herself was dark-haired and light-eyed, pretty, like the girl beside her, though neither seemed to fit very well the airy summer dresses they wore, as if both were shrinking as Farley grew. The camera caught the girl's long fine hair in a breeze, and she seemed to lean a little with it, slightly apart from her parents, unmoored, drifting. It was Jack. No Cardinals cap within a hundred miles. Did they know then, Tex wondered, that the mother was dying? Or was it something sudden, like a car crash? Behind them, in the photograph, arched over their heads like a personal banner, were the words WALT DISNEY WORLD.

"That's in Florida, isn't it?" he asked.

Behind her magazine, Jack nodded. "My grandpa lives down there."

"I went to Disney*land* once, but I bet this was better."

Her shrug made it clear she was no more anxious to talk about her dead mother than he was his bum hand. He took a swig and changed the subject. "It's a rip you can only practice with the team," he said. "You're better than most guys. Better than me, anyway, which isn't saying much."

Jack sighed. "You'll get good, Tex. Say what you want about Farley, he's a good coach."

Tex thought a moment. "What would I say?"

She lowered her magazine and turned to look out the window near the head of her bed. He hadn't noticed it before with all the clutter, but there in the window, suspended by string and suction cup, was the one detail remotely conforming to his idea of girl decor: a small glass cardinal. Sunlight passing through the ornament fell on her white pillowcase like a Kool-Aid spill.

Tex studied The Hand for a moment, warm and buzzing at

the end of his arm. "I like him," he said, decisively. "Your dad's okay."

Jack gave the glass cardinal a tweak, causing it to shimmy.

"Even so," Tex continued. "I might not play, either."

Jack cocked her head and blinked, theatrically doubting her ears. "What?"

"I mean, what's the fun, if you're not gonna be there?"

"I'll be there, dummy. Watching."

"So I'll watch with you."

"Then we'd be two losers watching Farley coach a bunch of idiots. I did that last summer and it's *boring*. You gotta play so I'll have a reason to watch." She lifted her magazine again, and he left her alone, retreating to his own room to lie on his bed and stare at the ceiling. He wanted to believe that his offer to sit out the season had come from someplace honorable, from some offended sense of fair play. But the truth was, outside of half-hour P.E. scrimmages with boys who picked girls for dodgeball before they picked him, Tex had never in his life belonged to a team. And he'd never had a fan.

"Think he'll take one today, Dad?"

"Course he will." Farley ramped off Interstate 70 and joined the traffic flowing into St. Louis. "At least one."

Tex sat up from the floor of the VW minibus, where he'd groggily spent the hot two-hour drive among baseball equipment and empty beer cans. "Take one what?" he asked. "Who?"

Farley glanced at Jack, and the two of them shrugged. Since leaving his mother's driveway, Tex had been treated to a thorough history of the St. Louis organization, beginning with the great St. Louis Browns of the 1880s. Yet now that he had a question about their glorious Redbirds, Jack and Farley abruptly clammed up.

He sat back in a funk while Farley embarked on a "secret shortcut" through the maze of the city, stopping and starting and taking so many turns that Tex felt like one of the beer cans rolling around at his feet. Finally, rejoining steadier, less clever traffic, Farley said, "Thar she blows!" and Tex moved forward for a look. Busch Stadium filled the windshield like an illusion, so enormous and stunning he caught his breath. The stadium rose above lesser buildings like a great multilayered concrete wedding cake. It put him in mind of the pyramids, or the Colosseum—an architectural wonder.

"Wow," was all he could say.

Farley drove once around the stadium before giving in to Jack's impatience and submitting to a five-dollar parking lot. "Bring my mitt," Jack told Tex, and they all spilled out into the hazy St. Louis sun. Hawkers tried to sell them pennants and caps and T-shirts, scalpers held fingers in the air, and everywhere Tex looked red-clad fans marched toward the gates like ants to sugar. Tex got his ticket punched and followed Farley into the stadium's antechamber, a soaring cavern jam-packed with the smells of damp concrete, popcorn, hot dogs, and beer.

Some minutes later, his jumbo dog cradled in Jack's mitt, Tex followed Farley and Jack up the ramp over a soft gravel of peanut shells and popcorn.

"Get ready, Tex," Farley said near the top. Sunlight and a

hum of voices poured in from a square opening in the concrete. Maybe it was just the darkness of the ramp, but the light seemed extraordinary to Tex, as if the sun itself bobbed just beyond the opening. The voices, too, seemed strange, a massive compilation of sound that reminded him of cicadas at dusk, erupting all at once into huge, organized song.

"For what?" he asked.

"For your first gander at one of America's great sights." Farley placed his beer hand in the small of Tex's back, prodding him forward with a single extended finger. "It'll never be the same again, Tex. After the first time, the sky is never so blue. And the grass, Jack?"

She rolled her eyes, but recited dutifully, "Never so green."

Then darkness exploded into blue, cement dropped from Tex's feet, and he was hovering above an expanse so purely, brilliantly green it made him dizzy. When he found his footing again, he saw that it was just an ordinary ball field, arranged in the usual geometry of infield, base path, and outfield, yet something about the height and the soaring canyon walls of human faces made it extraordinary, miraculous. He couldn't believe a player could do anything on such a field but stand there and grin.

They located their seats, just over the left-field wall, in time to sing "The Star-Spangled Banner." Farley sang loud, as if he'd come for no other reason, and Tex learned with amazement that, like his mother, his stepfather could carry a tune. When the song ended, Farley produced a cigar from his shirt pocket and artfully lit it; the game, Tex gathered, could now commence.

The Cardinal pitcher struck out the first two batters, and the third popped up to center field, and the crowd returned to its feet as the home team hustled in. A lone St. Louis player, made minuscule by distance, approached the plate, and the din of the crowd changed in pitch, honing itself to a low rhythmic chanting that sounded to Tex like "WHO? WHO? WHO?"

He turned to Jack and she leaned close. "Lou Brock!" she yelled—the player on her wall—and "WHO?" became "LOU!"

Farley leaned to yell behind Jack's back, "Whaddaya bet he takes the first pitch, Tex?"

Tex declined the bet, and Brock drove the ball through the gap between first and second base. The right fielder scooped up the ball and continued in, poised to throw. Brock rounded first and slowed, but didn't turn back, and he and the outfielder began what looked like a game of chicken—each daring the other to actually *do* something—before Brock gave up, finally, and trotted back to first. Tex wondered why the crowd was going so crazy for a lousy single. When the noise died down, he mustered the nerve to ask.

"Watch," Farley said.

Another Cardinal was at the plate, but the pitcher seemed more interested in Brock, who stood a couple of steps from first base—a lead you couldn't pick off with a rifle, even Tex knew. Yet the pitcher threw to first; Brock hopped back to the bag; the first baseman returned the ball to the pitcher and they began all over again. Farley chose the moment to treat Tex to a pop quiz. "How far is it to second, Tex?"

"Ninety feet."

At last the pitcher threw one toward the plate, and Brock, from an upright position, was suddenly closing on second. The catcher leaped to his feet and fired, but Brock was already dropping, sliding, rising safe on the base. The crowd went nuts.

"Ninety feet for you and me," Farley yelled. "For Lou Brock, three point two seconds!"

Jack pulled a pen from her pocket and scribbled something in her program. Tex bent to see.

"Number forty-one what?" he asked.

"Steals, dummy. He's stolen over fifty bases for nine seasons straight. The record's ten."

The Cardinal batter struck out swinging, and the crowd, at last, took their seats. Tex read the back of a fan's T-shirt several rows down:

BROCK'S
BASE BURGLARS
"105" CLUB

Again he turned to Jack. Maury Wills, she informed him, held the single-season record of 104 stolen bases, and some people thought this would be the year Brock broke it. "He's ahead of Wills's pace by ten games," Jack said.

"But don't forget, darlin'," Farley said, "Ol' Maury stole fifty-six in his last sixty-six games."

"So? Brock's stolen forty-one out of forty-six tries. That's like ninety percent—and it's only June."

Farley raised his palms. "I'm with ya, Jack. I just think it's a little early for T-shirts."

The next batter drove the ball all the way to the center-field wall, scoring Brock and beginning a trend that held until the only drama left, by the bottom of the sixth, was whether or not Brock would steal another base. He nearly cheated Jack and the rest of his fans with a hit that sailed over the right-field wall, just foul. Farley watched it go, whistling. "He's a hitter. Everybody thinks all he does is steal bases, but let me tell you. You gotta get on base to steal another. He'll hit three thousand before he's done."

Unimpressed, a relief pitcher nearly hit Brock in the head with his first throw.

"That's a duster, Tex," Farley said. "That'll keep any batter from digging in."

Brock adjusted his helmet and dug in. The pitcher threw a ball that swerved like a drunk, and Brock smashed it down the first-base line for his second single of the day. Another game of cat and mouse followed at first, before the pitcher finally pitched and Brock sprang. He beat the throw, and Tex's ears rang with the noise.

"Only nine to go for ten seasons straight!" Jack cried. "Sixty-four to beat Wills!" Farley added.

One foot on second, Brock turned to give the fans a sub-dued wave, then returned his attention to the mound; the pitcher was reading signals, and he had another base to steal.

In the top of the ninth, Tex had his final live glimpse of Lou Brock. A Philadelphia batter sent a line drive to left field, a sure double, when suddenly Brock exploded from position, his cleats a blur, and slid, as if sliding were the only natural culmination of any burst of speed, into a perfect intersection with the dropping ball. The game was over. The crowd took up its chant one more time, and Brock, clearly grateful, lobbed the ball over the left-field wall. Jack and Tex lunged to catch it with their mitts, but it fell short, into the hands of a fat man with a sunburned skull.

Jack cussed and looked ready to cry, but Farley told her to shake it off. After all, she'd seen one of the greats today. Brock would surely go on to break both records, and while that bald guy caught a mere baseball, Jack had witnessed history.

On their way out of the city, Tex thought of his father at Ebbets Field, how he'd watched Jackie Robinson endure outrageous insults from the Phillies; he thought how his stepsister was named after that ballplayer; and he thought how, today, twenty-seven years later, he'd sat beside her in another major-league ballpark watching Lou Brock steal bases from the descendants of those same Phillies. Farley was right, he thought. Baseball was history, like wars and presidents, and as they drove back to Iowa, Tex knew that in another twenty-seven years he'd still be able to recall the smell of Busch Stadium that day, the popcorn and hot dogs and peanut shells and beer and Farley's cigar. And he'd still be able to hear, clear as if she were standing beside him, Jack's twelve-year-old voice adding to the love song of "LOU LOU LOU."

5

After that, Tex was hooked. Farley raised a pitcher's mound down by the Archibald, Jack donned a scuffed Twins helmet, and Tex heaved ball after ball in the vicinity of her knees. They practiced all afternoon, stayed up late with the Cubs and Cards, and met again at the breakfast table, hungry for box scores.

Caroline began to worry.

"You're turning him into a fanatic," Tex heard her say, as he got out of bed to use the bathroom.

"So?" Farley said. "It's good for him. Gets his nose out of the books for a while."

Sunburned and bone-tired, his shoulder still twitching, Tex had to agree. He didn't feel at all like himself. He felt like a ballplayer.

"And into the sports page and baseball magazines," his mother said.

"No harm in that. Look at Jack."

"I have."

"Meaning? Never mind, I know. She's more worried about her swing than her hairstyle, so she's pretty messed up, right?"

"I wouldn't call what she is 'messed up,' exactly. She's got more sense than most adults I know. And I could care less about her hairstyle. I'm talking about her happiness."

There was a pause, then the sound of an empty beer can hitting the trash. "She's as happy as any twelve-year-old I ever knew," Farley said.

Tex's mother made a huffing sound, the same incredulous little cough he'd heard many times before, usually in response to some highly calm, infuriating thing his father had said. "She's lost her mother," Caroline said, "she's moved away from her friends, and now her daddy's found himself a real live son to play with. She's *ecstatic*."

"That's the wine talking."

"Any time I hit a nerve, it's the wine talking."

They were silent a minute, before Farley groaned with rising and announced he was going to bed. "You coming?"

"No," Caroline said. "I'm not sleepy. Or anything else."

"Fine." The floor trembled with Farley's approach, and Tex just made it back to his room.

Some time later, throwing perfect strikes in his dreams, Tex jerked awake. His door was open and someone was there—a large figure, a pale mass just standing there, filling the frame of his door, scratching idly at a full moon of belly. Then, suddenly, the figure gave a salute. "Sorry, sports fans, thought this was the head," he said, and turned, and shut the door with barely a sound.

The next day, on reprieve from practice, Tex and Jack followed the Archibald to the Mississippi, a weedy, indirect march of several miles. The river was still swollen from spring rains, yet they'd no sooner reached the bluffs before Jack punched him in the arm and challenged him to a swim race to the other side. Illinois, she declared, couldn't be any more boring than Iowa. Tex watched an entire tree float by, branches curled over brown water like a bird's foot, like a drowned crow, and said he'd pass. He pointed out the visible evidence of undercurrents, cycloning eddies that would suck a body down like a flushed goldfish.

"You're just chicken," Jack said.

"Of you?" he said. "I'd whup you one-handed."

"And when you lost, that'd be why." Jack made a crybaby face. " 'No fair, Jack, you got two good hands!' "

Tex spat over the edge of the bluffs, into water. "Least I can throw a strike."

"You think so, huh?"

Tex shrugged. "I don't see *you* pitching for Farley." The second he said it, he wanted to take it back, but it was too late. Jack turned and shoved him, so hard he fell backward into brambles and thorns. "Screw you, Donleavy."

Tex fought the bush wildly, ripping his T-shirt, and emerged with a spastic left hook that clipped the bill of her Cardinals cap, lifted it, spun it over the edge and into the river.

"My cap!" she cried.

"Shouldn't have pushed me."

"I gotta get it!"

Tex looked at the cap, moving duck-swift downstream. "Sorry, Jack. It's a goner."

"You idiot! You one-handed freak! That's my Cardinals cap!" She pushed him aside and ran along the bluffs, and Tex followed, wincing through branches. She came to a part in the rocks and took it down, quick as a monkey. Tex followed, somewhat less nimbly, and emerged on a sandbar he'd never seen before, a secret beach. Jack sprinted across the sand, grabbed up a long stick of deadwood, and splashed knee-deep into the river.

For a moment, still feeling the lash of her insult, Tex didn't care if she drowned. When it occurred to him that if she drowned, Farley would never forgive him, he stepped toward the water.

"Jack," he said. "Don't."

"Shut up!"

The cap came along and she took another step, staggering against the current, extending the stick. Water shoved against her waist and the stick trembled and it was almost funny, Tex thought, how much she looked like a stick herself, like one more twiggy thing the river would carry off.

Then she took another step and it wasn't funny at all.

"Jack!" he blurted. "Let it go. I'll get you a new one."

"I don't want a new one."

"Then let's follow it. It'll wash up on its own."

She stretched herself, the stick, as far as she could. The cap drifted closer, spinning in circles. It hit the tip of the stick, bowed it, and had begun to pull free when she lifted the stick, stabbed, and managed to hook the hole at the back. She eased the cap from the water, a limp red fish.

She twisted to show him. "My cap, Tex. Ain't *never* gonna lose it. It's magic!"

"So magic it about made you disappear. Now get back here."

She grabbed the cap and let the stick go; it floated off quick—like her smile.

"What's the matter, Jack?"

"Can't move."

"Sure you can. Turn around and take a step." Tex's own feet were cold and he looked down to discover he'd waded in up to his shins.

"Can't, Tex. Only thing keeping me here is mud. Pull my feet lose, I'm gone."

"Hold on, I'll get another stick."

"No!" she snapped. "Don't move. Don't leave."

Tex didn't know if he'd ever seen real fear on a real face, but Jack's expression convinced him he hadn't.

"Okay," he said, "I'm not moving. Here . . ." He took a step and reached with his good hand, but a yardstick would not have made up the difference. He took another step.

"Careful, Tex. No sense in us both going."

"Nobody's going anywhere. Hand me the cap."

Jack reached back with the cap, and Tex began to take an- other step when something under the water struck his knee and knocked him off balance, left him stumbling in water. He regained his footing, but now he was facing the wrong way, his good hand to shore, his bad hand to Jack. Another step

57

anywhere seemed impossible, and he understood her fear: the river had them.

"You okay?" she asked.

"Yeah. Now hand it here."

Jack reached with her cap and Tex reached with The Hand, forcing the fingers to be longer, stretching until he thought he felt tearing at the joints, straining until at last he saw, more than he felt, the cap beneath his fingertips, and he clenched.

"Got it?" Jack asked.

"Think so. You?"

"Oh, yeah."

"Then let's go." He pulled, Jack stepped, and they stumbled backward in the water, thrashed a moment in the current, and finally lunged, together, for shore.

They crawled over silt and flopped onto their backs, their limbs strewn like driftwood. Tex lay there catching his breath and thinking about *Lord of the Flies*, about kids washing up onshore. He rolled his head to look at Jack—and looked quickly away.

How many times, he wondered, would he find himself alone with Jack Dickerson in a soaking-wet T-shirt?

She turned her face his way, but Tex kept his eyes on the sky. "Thanks," she said. "Saved my butt."

The comment entered his ear and became a kind of roar, like the ocean in a conch. He must have river water in there, he figured.

The Mississippi rushed on.

"Tex?" Jack said after a moment.

"What?"

"Sorry. About what I said."

Tex took a deep breath. "Me too. About what I said. I didn't mean it."

Far from shore, a fish splashed with the sound of a skipped stone.

"Jack?" Tex said.

"Yeah?"

"Here." He handed her the magic cap, and together they freed it from his purple fingers.

6

With Busch Stadium still vivid in his mind, Tex's heart sank at the sight of where he himself would play ball. The Lee County Ballpark was not one brilliant, perfectly shaped field but rather three imperfectly shaped ones out in the middle of farmland, a grass-and-dirt pie cut into thirds with a flimsy crust of snow-drift fence all around. Each diamond came with a backstop, a bench beyond either baseline, and a stand of aluminum bleachers with a maximum weight capacity of twelve Iowa farm ladies, tops.

Well, he reminded himself, you had to start somewhere, and the first base Lou Brock ever stole was probably a piece of cardboard. Or a paperback book.

Since Farley's minibus brought both equipment and coach, it was easy for Tex to spot his new teammates: they were the ones not yet huddled around an adult or warming up in a line of partners that reminded him of the Virginia reel. They were the ones loafing in the bleachers, a dozen or so T-shirted boys fussing with mitts and watching his approach from the shade of their caps. Tex thought he recognized the shoulders of one big kid and prayed he was wrong.

"Drop that duffel and have a seat, son," Farley said when they reached the bleachers. "You too, Jack." The Twins made room for them at the far end of the lowest row, and from there Tex watched Farley pull out a fresh cigar and light it with great, excruciating patience.

"To those of you returning to the Twins," he began at last, "I'm proud to have you back. To the rookies, like Tex here—"

"Tex?" someone said.

Tex looked over, knowing the voice went with the shoulders he'd recognized: Joey Dunsmore, the troglodyte who'd yelled at him and Melanie Bloom that last day of school, sitting now at the other end of the row, wearing a Twins cap. Pointing a bat.

"You mean ol' Davy Donleavy, there, Coach?" Dunsmore said, and the rest of the team followed the bat.

Tex watched a pheasant land in a distant soybean field.

Farley took a puff on his cigar. He shrugged. "What you call each other is your business, Mr. Dunce-more."

A burst of snorts and giggles followed, but Tex stayed out of it; he knew a safety-in-numbers laugh when he heard one— as he knew, without looking, that Dunsmore was watching him, that dopey grin on his face, his knuckles tight around the neck of the bat.

Farley got back to business. He grabbed his clipboard and took roll, allowing everyone but Jack to identify himself with a raised hand. At one kid's hearty "Here, Coach," Tex got his first look at Andrew Ferguson, the shortstop Farley had won with a full house. He was the one among them who looked put out by the act of sitting. His feet jittered, and he tirelessly ground a baseball into the meat of his glove. He chewed gum as if his jaw were motorized.

Farley dropped the clipboard and faced his team. "Now listen up. I know some of your names from last year; the rest of you, don't have a cow if I say, 'Hey, you' "—he pointed, startling a tubby kid with glasses—"till I learn your name."

"Louis Wrigley," the kid said.

"Doublemint or Juicy Fruit?" Farley let the kid squirm a while before winking. "Just messin' with you, Wrig. Now. Those of you who were with me last year know the drill, but for the rookies it works like this." And he outlined his no-favorites, no-pampering philosophy of coaching twelve-year-old boys: You want to play second base? Be the best second baseman on the squad. Same for left field, same for pitching.

A kid named Zimmerman raised his hand. "Everyone gets to play, though, right? My dad says that's the rule." His hair was the reddest Tex had ever seen in real life.

Farley grinned. "Everyone gets to play, Red. Wouldn't be any fun otherwise, would it? That's why we have a thing called position rotation, which allows for certain players to switch off with others on the field, so everybody, at some point, gets to get dirty."

Zimmerman looked dubious, and Tex couldn't blame him. Despite rules and promises, Tex knew that a kid like Zimmerman, who reminded him of himself, would spend much of the summer on the bench.

Farley wondered aloud, somewhat ominously, if there were any *more* questions before they began, and Dunsmore raised his paw.

"Yeah, Coach. Uh—" He thumbed in Tex's direction. "I see you brung your daughter, there, along with Donleavy."

Farley waited, his cigar twitching.

"Well, I just wanted to know . . ." Dunsmore stirred loose dirt with his bat, as if the words were hiding there. "Heck, Coach. We don't haveta play with no girl, too, do we?"

"That fat, ignorant, turd-brained jerk," Tex seethed as he headed for the outfield.

"Get used to it, Tex," Jack said, then left him for her place in the opposite line of partners. To their right, Ferguson had paired up with the lumpy kid named Wrigley, who was having trouble with the mechanics of his throw. Ferguson didn't seem to mind; he pounced on the erratic tosses and whipped them back, saying, "Don't sweat it, Wrig, just keep throwin', it'll come back."

"Hey, Davy!" To his left, Dunsmore gunned a ball at a kid named Rummelhart. "Helluva way to get on the team." He grinned at Jack.

"Shut up, Duncemore," Tex said.

"Okay, Davy." He caught Rummelhart's toss and returned it, as Tex did Jack's. "Hey," he persisted, "does this mean you're done with Melanie Bloom?"

Jack held the ball a moment, watching Tex. Tex said to Dunsmore, "You're some genius, you know that? *She*," he said, enunciating very carefully, "is my *stepsister*." He was so busy with his sarcasm he wasn't ready for Jack's next throw, a hard one-hopper that hit him in the shin.

Dunsmore guffawed. "She throws like it."

Tex rubbed his leg and tried to remember what his father had said about Jackie Robinson, something about having more dignity than pride. Or was it more guts than pride? Whatever it was, he'd made up his mind to be more like Jackie, when Jack dropped her mitt and marched toward Dunsmore.

"Whoa, here comes trouble." Dunsmore took a step back in mock fear, but also readied himself, Tex saw, for some genuine threat, some kind of sneaky, tomboy kung fu, possibly. He looked like a kid who knew what it felt like to be kicked in the crotch by a girl.

Jack didn't kick. She stopped at his big rubber cleats and looked up, curiously, into the shadow of his cap.

"If it was my birthday and I had one wish," she said, "know what it'd be?"

"That your dad never met his mom?"

She smiled, as if he were close. "Actually, I'd wish that you could have the brains to understand, for just one second, what a complete butt-wipe you are."

His grin withered to a hard, pale line. He stepped chest to chest with her, but she didn't budge.

Tex looked around for Farley, saw him setting the infield with rubber plates, head down and oblivious. None of the other boys made a move, and Tex knew he'd have to. He took two steps and stood next to Jack.

"Don't even think about it, Davy," Dunsmore said. "I don't fight girls, but I'll gladly knock your one-hand ass over the fence."

Now boys began drifting over. They glanced to the infield, but when they saw Farley wasn't paying attention, they turned to Tex, and he knew that the longer he just stood there doing nothing, the smaller and more deformed he became.

"Oh, yeah?" he said at last. His mouth was dry as wind.

Dunsmore smirked and gave him a push. "Why don't you go back to your books, Davy?"

"Why don't you go to hell?"

Dunsmore didn't even bother to remove his mitt, and by the looks of his fist, a tight bag of rocks cocked shoulder-high, he wouldn't need to. Tex kept his hands down, knowing his only victory would be in taking his beating like a man. And here came Dunsmore to give it to him.

"Knock it off already, will ya?"

An arm came between the boys. It was Andrew Ferguson's.

"Stay outta this, rook," Dunsmore said.

Ferguson stared at Dunsmore, icy, his jaw still—then suddenly grinned. Gum snapped between his molars. "Outta what? Ya had it coming, ya big dope."

"Who's a dope?"

"Aw, cripes." He shook his head and smiled at Jack, but she kept her eyes on Dunsmore, and Dunsmore kept his eyes on Ferguson, until Farley broke it all up by yelling, finally, for everybody to hustle in. Tex jogged in with the rest of the team, fighting a hot, breathless sense of failure. He remembered now exactly what his father had said about Jackie Robinson. But his father was wrong, he thought bitterly. Sometimes pride was more important than dignity, and guts meant throwing your fist into somebody's face.

Farley barked out positions and sent the team off to fill

them as if he hadn't seen or heard a thing. But then Tex saw him give Jack a smile and a swat on her way to first base, and he understood: by not interfering, Farley had not only demonstrated his no-favorites rule, he'd allowed his daughter to be a ballplayer.

Tex alone had failed the test.

His reward was a trip to right field, where he watched in a funk as Farley coached the kid named Rummelhart in checking ghost runners, throwing the slider, and reading Wrigley's chubby little fingers behind the plate. Other Twins answered gamely as Farley bellowed out questions. "Third base! Big D! Where you going with this grounder, no outs and a runner on second?" He grounded Rummelhart's pitch to Dunsmore, who knelt, scooped, checked the runner at second, and threw to first. Jack stretched to meet the ball, then showed her willingness to throw out the phantom runner should he be dumb enough to try.

"Good eye, Jack. Good look. This is a *thinking* game, boys and girls. Never stop thinking and the execution will follow. Right field! Runner on second, one out, lefty in the box!" Farley stepped to the other side of the plate and reversed his grip on the bat. "Here comes a Texas leaguer for Tex—where's he gonna go?" Rummelhart pitched and Farley looped one over Jack's head. She ran for it, but Tex got there first, grabbed it bare-handed, and threw. The ball landed at Dunsmore's feet.

"Whoo-whee!" Farley called. "Kid's got a gun, but the runner is *safe*! Center field! Two outs, runners on the corners!" Rummelhart pitched and Farley ripped the ball through the middle of the infield. Or not quite through. Ferguson lay stretched out on the base path, his mitt high, the ball pinched in its lips.

"Snowconed my best damn swing, you little frog! Damn." He stepped from the plate to shake it off. "Okay, that's enough of that. Let's see some bats. Right field, get in here and toss a few to Wrig. Rum, grab the helmets."

Jack gave Tex a quick smile as he passed first base, and Wrigley threw him a ball. The catcher nodded, slugged his mitt once, and showed Tex the strike.

His first pitch sailed so high it almost cleared the backstop.

"Nice and easy for now, Tex," Farley counseled. "Find your center and just put 'em in there. Don't worry about power."

Tex took a breath, stretched, and delivered the next pitch cleanly into Wrigley's mitt. Then another, adding speed. When he'd completed five consecutive strikes, Farley called for a hitter. Dunsmore grabbed his bat. He jammed a helmet over his ears and stepped into the box.

"Steady as she goes, pitcher," Farley said. He hovered umpire-style over Wrigley's shoulder. "Just put it over the plate."

As the team waited, Tex tried to ignore his hatred for Dunsmore, to simply follow Farley's advice and put one over the plate. But there was that idiotic grin, those dopey dark eyes daring him to try to get one past his wagging bat. Tex remembered the last day of school, the dimples in Melanie Bloom's cheeks, the rotten things he himself had said to her—and he pitched.

Something cracked and he watched the ball sizzle over

Ferguson's mitt, climb a blue sky, linger awhile with the sun, then drop, soundlessly, into the soybean field. When Tex turned back to the plate, Dunsmore was grinning like Dracula.

Farley whistled. "Good swing, Big D. Tex, good pitch, right down Broadway, but big as a house. Put a little wrinkle in it this time, son, like we practiced."

Wrigley produced another ball and Tex tried the slider Farley had taught him. Dunsmore whipped it down the third-base line, trimming grass. He obliterated three more pitches, two of them obvious balls, before Farley intervened.

"Okay, that's good wood, Big D, but don't let me see you swinging at some of those turkeys in a game. Got me?"

"Gotcha, Coach."

Tex stepped from the mound, anxious for the grass of right field—but Farley stopped him. "Not so fast, lefty. Let's see how you fare against mere boys. Frogman! You're up."

Ferguson hustled in, took the helmet from Dunsmore, and grabbed a bat. Gum snapped and popped. He tapped dirt from his cleats, dusted his palms, and stepped into the box. His stance was all tight rubber and steel coils, and Tex knew his best pitch would look to this kid about as imposing as a beach ball.

He read Wrigley's signs, and was attempting to locate his center when Jack spoke.

"No sweat, Tex," she said from first base. All the Twins looked over.

Tex kept his eyes on Ferguson, watched him blend into a red haze.

"Just like at home, now," she went on. "Just pitch it in there."

The haze slowly lifted and Tex saw that Ferguson had stepped out of the box to stare at first base. Now he stepped back in, but something had changed in his stance; it was less compact, somehow, with a strike zone you could pull a car into.

Tex wanted to pitch before it changed back. He wound up and aimed for the outside corner. Ferguson swung, and the ball found Wrigley's mitt.

"That's a strike," Farley said.

"Good pitch, Tex," someone behind him said. "Attaboy, Tex. Way to put 'em in there."

Ferguson shook his head and pounded the plate once with the bat. He faced Tex again, showed him where he wanted it—then watched a fastball raise dust from Wrigley's mitt.

Farley showed a fist. "That's two. C'mon now, Frog. I know you got wood."

Tex delivered his next pitch with the rubber-armed joy of knowing exactly where it was going. It found Wrigley's mitt once more, and Andrew Ferguson struck out swinging. He spit out his wad of gum, grabbed his glove, and jogged back to short, Farley watching him all the way, chewing on his cigar, saying nothing.

Rummelhart whiffed at Tex's next two pitches, then caught the scalp of the third, a grounder that got by Tex but not Ferguson, who scooped it up, stepped on second, and flung it to first. Jack caught it, then held her pose a moment—foot on the rubber base, arm stretched out to meet the ball—savoring.

Twins hooted for the double play, Farley called, "Attaway, infield!" and Tex was just hungry enough to stay on the mound, to pitch for Farley's Minnesota Twins, that he could see nothing in Ferguson's lingering smile toward first base—toward Jack—than the sheer joy of a good play.

7

Tex awoke the next day to a sun-swamped room and the nagging, thick-headed feeling he'd overslept something big.

Caroline was in the kitchen, attacking a legal pad with her pencil while Willa May blunted a fat orange Crayola on linoleum.

"Where is everybody?" he asked.

They both kept writing. "Good morning," his mother said.

Tex looked out the window, toward the Archibald. "They go somewhere?"

"Last I knew, Farley was in the garage, working on the mower. And Jack"—she gave a tremendous stretch—"has gone to a matinee."

"Matinee?" The word felt like bits of gravel in Tex's mouth.

"At the Galaxy. A boy from your team stopped by—Andrew something? They waited to see if you were ever gonna wake up, till they could wait no longer. They said to tell you they'd catch up with you later."

Tex wandered out into hard sunlight, letting the screen door slam behind him. Farley was in the garage, down on one knee, prodding the Lawn-Boy with a screwdriver. He glanced at Tex's toes and said, "Hey, slugger. How's the arm today?"

"Did you know Ferguson was here?"

"Frog? What'd he want?"

"Jack."

Farley looked up.

"They went to a movie," Tex said.

"Why didn't you go with them?"

Tex shrugged. "Didn't feel like it."

Farley cranked the mower, and they both stood back as it coughed black smoke from its lungs, then died.

"Balls," Farley said.

"How come you named her after a ballplayer?"

"Who, Jack?" He shrugged. "Seemed like somebody ought to. Would've done the same to a boy, too, if she'd been one."

"Her mom didn't mind?"

"Jack's ma? She was a good sport, back when we were first married."

Tex stared at his own two big toes; between them, a large black ant raced back and forth. "She's kind of tough to figure. Jack."

Farley swallowed beer and checked his watch. "What's so tough to figure?"

"I don't know. She just seems sometimes kind of . . ."

"Smart-mouthed?"

"Well, yeah. But also . . ." A word was on his mind, but he

hesitated to use it, thinking it would sound unmanly. He recalled the conversation he'd overheard between Farley and his
mother, and said it anyway. "Unhappy."

Farley looked out at the yard and sighed. "I was afraid of
that. She shows a pretty brave face around me, but I was
afraid, other times, she might still be missing her mom."

When he didn't elaborate, Tex asked, "When did she die?"

"Two years ago this fall."

Tex was shocked. He'd assumed Jack's mom had died
when Jack was a little girl. He'd thought it would require
many years alone with Farley to turn a little girl into Jack
Dickerson. He recalled the photograph on her desk and wondered at his stupidity: her mother was holding a baby in that
picture, the same one who was now in his mother's kitchen,
drawing on the floor. Willa May was the proof of a recent
death, and the girl in that picture, whom he'd taken to be a
much younger Jack, was really the same rough tomboy who'd
shoved him into thorns by the river. It wasn't the long-term
absence of her mother that had done this to her, any moron
could see, but the recent, abrupt removal.

"How'd it happen?" he asked.

Farley slapped his neck. "Unpleasantly." He observed the
smear of blood between his fingers, then wiped it on his shirt.
"She'd always been frail, but when she started hitting the
bottle . . ." He shook his head.

Instinctively Tex looked over his shoulder to see if his
mother was in earshot. She wasn't, but even so it seemed Farley might've kept his voice down. Tex bent over and took hold
of the crank handle on the mower.

"Can I try?"

"To hell with the lawn," Farley grumbled. "Let's grab a couple of mitts, kiddo, and I'll teach you the curveball."

After the pitching lesson, Farley drove off in the minibus to meet some buddies, and Tex stationed himself in front of the Cubs on TV, determined not to move until Jack got back from the matinee. Two minutes later, he jumped up to grab a bag of Ruffles from the kitchen.

"Hey, baby," his mother said.

"Hey."

He carried the chips back to the TV and dug in. He would not move again, not even after she got home. He could sit there all afternoon. All *night*, if he wanted to.

He got thirsty.

"Good game?" Caroline was helping Willa May fit wooden barnyard shapes into obvious places. Tex grabbed a Coke from the fridge and checked the clock. "It's okay."

"Who's winning?"

"Cubs," he said.

"Cubs," she repeated, making the word sound like itself, not like a baseball team. She reached and composed, with her fingertips, the tangle of curls on Willa May's forehead. "Jack should be home soon," she said, as if only to remind herself, but Tex seized the opportunity to demonstrate his complete indifference by returning to the game.

He was back in eight minutes, looking for ice.

"Tex, you're up and down like a grasshopper. What's bugging you?"

"Nothing."

"Are you bored?"

"No. I'm watching the game."

"You're watching, but you're not."

"Well," he said, suddenly flustered, "who can pay attention with all the quiet around here? Farley's not yelling at the players, Jack's not explaining every play, this kid hasn't screamed *once* all day. I might as well read a book!"

She let him have his fit, then said, somewhat dreamily, "They do kind of grow on you, don't they."

Tex pulled out a chair and sat down heavily. "They're nuts, Ma. I'm sorry, but they are."

She shrugged and sipped from her coffee mug. Tex watched her, wanting to ask if wine made living with such people any easier. "We probably seem strange to them, too," she said after a moment. "Don't you think?"

Tex thought about it. "Maybe. But—and I'm not saying I don't *like* 'em or anything. It's just. I mean . . ."

"You're wondering how I could go from a man like your father to a man like Farley?"

Tex nodded, more relieved than amazed by her ESP.

Caroline took a breath and let it out slow. She peered into the coffee mug. "You're still young, Tex, but we don't need to pretend you don't understand a thing or two about being alone." She looked up, placed a cool palm over The Hand. She left it there just long enough to make him think he was going to burst out bawling, then removed it. "Your father's a good man in many ways, but he wasn't especially good for me, or me for him, and when he asked for the divorce—"

"He asked for it?"

"Baby, I thought you knew that much."

Tex stared at the table. "I guess I did."

Now it was time for his bangs to be adjusted. "Anyway," she resumed, "I was hurt. For a long time. Now, I know Farley's no prince of good breeding like your father"—she smiled to let him know her sarcasm wasn't completely hostile—"but he took to me like a big old mutt, and I guess I needed that, that headlong, clumsy affection, more than I needed another purebred retriever." She took another sip and sat there staring just to Tex's left, as if remembering events from the distant past, as if all that clumsy headlong affection had long ago become a bothersome canine slobbering—or worse, dried up altogether. In any case Tex knew she wasn't telling him everything, as he knew he had no business knowing everything, as he knew, in his gut, he didn't *want* to know everything.

"And that's pretty much all I can tell you," she concluded. "Except for one crucial, top-secret thing."

"What?"

"Promise you won't let it change your opinion of him?"

He promised.

"He sang to me."

"He sang to you."

"He sang to me, Tex."

"You mean, like, outside your window? What did he sing, the national anthem?"

"Not outside my window, not the anthem. He sang a song, very quietly, into my left ear. I don't guess you'd understand what a little thing like that might mean to your creaky old mom, but you'd be well advised to remember the strategy."

76

They sat a moment watching Willa May struggle with a blocky pink pig. Outside, Tex thought he heard the sound of Jack's approach, the distinct cadence of bicycle chain rubbing chain guard, but the sound grew weaker, not stronger, and he turned back to his mother.

"What was the song?"

" 'She Thinks I Still Care.' " She smiled, a sudden wetness in her blue eyes. "Would you like to hear it?"

"Sure."

She cleared her throat, closed her eyes, and in a voice that rose and fell with the corny lilt of TV cowboys, she began to sing. Willa May became still as a puzzle piece and did not move again until the song was over, when she pointed a wooden horse toward the screen door.

"Wack," she said.

Tex and Caroline turned, waited for her to come in, but Jack just stood there, hand on the latch, staring in, watching something only she could see.

8

The day before the season opener, Farley gave Tex and Jack the afternoon off; if Tex wasn't ready for a real game by now, he by God never would be.

They didn't argue; they jumped on their bikes and rode toward town, leaving their gloves behind.

Tex's Schwinn Typhoon was an old two-speed kickback with the braking mechanism in the pedals; Jack's Huffy, a three-speed with handle brakes and a cardinal-red banana seat. Pedestrians moving along Big River sidewalks made good obstacles in a game of follow-the-leader, but after enough threats Tex and Jack ditched the bikes and sauntered into Manny's Barbershop. Manny gave them the eye over his newspaper, then continued reading. Tex popped dimes in the cooler and extracted sweating bottles of Coke.

"You boys got appointments?" Manny was a dark, skull-faced man with a fancy goatee that made you think, if you didn't know better, that he'd come straight from Chicago or

New York City, someplace crawling with nightclubs and jazz. In fact he'd grown up right there in Big River and had taken over the barbershop when his father died.

Jack caught Tex's eye—you *boys?*—and they both smiled. "No, sir," Tex said. "Just coolin' off."

"No haircuts, then."

"Thanks anyway."

"Thanks anyway," Manny said. "Son of a lawyer ought to know good grooming. You think your daddy is facing that jury today with a shaggy hat? No sir, got himself a fine proper gentleman's cut first thing this morning right here in this chair. Jury take one look at that cut, they *know* the truth."

Satisfied he was finished, Jack and Tex turned to the window. "What is he talking about?" she whispered.

"One of my dad's cases. He's in trial today."

"A murder trial? Like Charlie Manson? Remember those pictures in that book—where you couldn't see the *bodies* but you could see all the blood and knives and stuff? And that pregnant girl, with a *fork*—"

"No," Tex said, "not a murder trial."

"Oh." She turned back to the window. Across the street at the Galaxy Theater a line had formed for the matinee showing of *Blazing Saddles*. "Let's go see it," Jack said.

Tex stared sullenly at the theater, wondering if Andrew Ferguson was in there, wondering if Jack had planned on meeting him all along.

"I heard it's not *that* funny."

Jack nodded at the line. "That ain't what they heard."

"Yeah, well . . ." He searched his brain. "It's rated R."

"So? Look at all those kids. They'd let my little sister in there."

"So it's prohibited."

"It's what?"

"I'm not allowed to go to R movies by myself."

"You're not by yourself."

He made a face, unamused.

"Hell's bells, Tex—"

Manny rattled his paper, and Jack lowered her voice. "Heck, Tex. Farley lets me see whatever I want."

He met her stare. Now and then he liked nothing better than to forget one of his father's mandates, but Jack's challenge was less a bid for the next phase of entertainment as it was a commentary on the character of fathers. Since the beginning of summer hers had commanded the spotlight: Farley coached Little League and cracked jokes and took them to ball games. Tex didn't guess she'd be much impressed by a father who studied lawbooks and wore ties in the summer—even if he was, as people liked to say, the finest trial lawyer between the Mississippi and the Missouri. Tex was always greeted with smiles and left-handed handshakes in the corridors of the Lee County Courthouse, one place, his father assured him, he was free to haunt, as no harm could possibly come from a boy's unguided exposure to due process.

Jack sighed, and Tex watched her watching underage kids disappear into the Galaxy.

He drained his Coke and filed the bottle in the crate on the floor. "All right, then," he said. "Let's go."

"To the movie?"

"Forget the movie, will ya?" he said, and pushed through the door.

The Lee County Courthouse was an imposing, elderly structure of red brick and arched windows expressly designed, it seemed, to discourage the approach of minors. Tex and Jack dumped their bikes and scrambled up limestone steps. One of two massive wooden doors strained open, dousing them in cool air that was not air-conditioning but the ancient chill, Tex liked to think, you'd find in the bellies of the pyramids. On their way up marble stairs, Jack shook her head. "I don't see how a man could rape his girlfriend if she really was his girlfriend."

"It all depends on consent," Tex said. They came to the closed oak doors of District Court A. Beyond, a woman was speaking in a shaky voice, and Tex wondered if his father had already begun his cross-examination of Lucinda Barnes, the waitress from the Route 61 Diner. He whispered, "If she doesn't give her consent to, you know, *it*—"

"Screwing?"

Tex's neck burned and he turned from her, hating the tender-eared dork she was always turning him into. He took refuge in the slight gap between the oak doors, gaining a view of the jury box and the bench, but not the witness stand. The woman had stopped speaking, and now the entire court seemed to be listening to her sniffling.

"If she doesn't give consent," he whispered, trying to re-member how his father had put it, "and the man *makes* her, then it's rape no matter what, unless they're married. The jury just has to decide if she gave consent or not. Come on." He eased open the door and Jack followed him in.

They made their way to the middle of the back row, inconveniencing several sets of knees, and sat down. The jury box featured six men and six women, all twelve pairs of eyes fixed on Lucinda Barnes. Her red hair, Tex noted, was not in its usual ponytail but flowed freely from her head, splashing the shoulders of a white blouse. Seeing her here, outside the diner, was strange, like seeing Ms. Riley outside Taft Elementary.

Lucinda Barnes blew her nose into a hankie. Above and to her left, Judge Tanner bided his time. His silver hair always looked to Tex as if he'd just rolled up his car window, and his teeth were yellow, but he liked to bend down when he saw Tex carrying some book and say, "Mr. Donleavy, sir, you are a gentleman and a scholar," so Tex liked him. Now the judge nodded in the direction of one of two tables, and a man stood up.

"That's my dad," Tex said, his heart suddenly pounding.

"Nice haircut," said Jack. "Who's the other guy?" Their view of Jacob's client was limited to the back of the man's carefully combed head and a navy-blue jacket his father had paid two dollars for, Tex guessed, at the Salvation Army in Burlington. "The defendant," he said. "Ray Stucky."

Jacob walked to within a few feet of the jury box, then faced the stand. "If you're ready, Miss Barnes, I'd like to continue."

She blew once more into the hankie. "I'm ready."

Jacob gave her a friendly smile. "I'd like to ask you a few questions, if I may, about your residence."

She nodded.

82

"You live alone at number two Maple Street?"

She nodded again, and Jacob let Judge Tanner correct her. "Answer yes or no, please," the judge said.

"Yes," she said.

"And you like your landlady, Mrs. Reeves."

"Yes."

"Her apartment is right next to yours."

"Yes."

"She's a kind woman."

"Yes."

"If you get locked out, or lose your keys, she's always happy to let you in."

"Yes."

The court was lulled with yeses, and Jack gave Tex a nudge. "This how he talks at home?"

Tex leaned to whisper. "You gotta picture you're in a long hallway with the witness, and there's all these doors she can get out of. Each question closes a door. That's what he calls it: closing the doors."

Jack sighed and turned back to watch.

"On the night of March tenth, then," Jacob continued, "when Mrs. Reeves heard you screaming that you didn't want Mr. Stucky to leave—"

"Objection, Your Honor." A man stood, gave a tug to the lapels of his jacket. "Mrs. Reeves said she *thought* that's what she heard. Counsel's question is a misstatement of the record." This was Tom Gray, the new county attorney, recently imported from Des Moines. He was, as Tex's father put it, an ambitious young man.

The judge sustained the objection. "Stick to the facts, Jacob."

"All right," he said agreeably. "Miss Barnes, it is a fact, isn't it, that you had a relationship with Mr. Stucky?"

"Yes."

"A sexual relationship."

"Yes."

"And it's a fact that you yourself installed the security lock on the inside of your door."

"Yes."

"And you did this, you say, to keep Ray Stucky out. Because he had a key to the other lock. A key you had duplicated just for him."

Lucinda Barnes stiffened. "No," she said. "I had a key made, but not for him. He stole it."

Jacob looked confused. "You had a duplicate key made for yourself? With Mrs. Reeves right next door?"

"Your Honor," Mr. Gray said, "does counsel intend to argue the right of a single woman to duplicate keys for her own convenience and safety?"

Jack whispered, "What's the big deal with the key?"

"If she's lying about the key," Tex said, "she could be lying about everything."

Judge Tanner did not glance up from a note he was making. "Overruled."

Jacob stepped toward the jury box, then turned again to the witness. "Well, let's forget the key for the moment. Let's talk about the lock. Which you say you installed yourself. Using, I imagine, a screwdriver?"

"Yes."

"And of course drilling pilot holes."

"No."

Jacob wasn't walking, but he leaned forward as if he'd suddenly stopped. "You didn't drill pilot holes?"

"I don't own a drill."

"So you screwed six one-inch screws into solid oak by hand? You must have very strong wrists, Miss Barnes."

"Now what?" Jack wanted to know, and the State agreed.

"Your Honor . . ." Mr. Gray complained. The judge advised Jacob to get on with it.

"Of course," he said. "So there you were, Miss Barnes, on the night of March tenth, your door double-locked, watching TV."

"Yes."

"You kept the volume low so as not to disturb Mrs. Reeves."

"Yes."

"You made some popcorn."

"Yes."

"But you didn't get ready for bed."

"That's right."

"You didn't undress."

"No."

"You wore a T-shirt and jeans."

"That's right."

"And underpants."

"Yes," she answered flatly, without the slightest trace of blush. And for each of her yeses, Tex noticed, Ray Stucky had a slight shake of the head.

"And you fell asleep on the couch."

"Yes."

"And you say the next thing you knew, Mr. Stucky was in the room. You say you tried to scream, but he put a hand over your mouth. You say he ripped your T-shirt with one hand over your mouth. You say he undid your jeans and pulled them down with one hand over your mouth, wrestled you onto your stomach, pulled down your underpants, undid his trousers, and sexually violated you—all with one hand over your mouth."

"Yes."

"That's your testimony?"

"Yes," she said in a steady voice, "it is."

Tex ventured a glance to his left. Jack's eyes were wide, her mouth slightly agape as if she were standing in that apartment, watching. As for himself, he could not deny the unpleasant fact of his arousal, a shameful little fire Lucinda Barnes's wet eyes did nothing to extinguish. He was beginning to wish they'd gone to *Blazing Saddles* after all.

Jacob was nodding, as if impressed with the witness. "Very well, Miss Barnes," he said. "Let's go back to the lock. You know how it was broken."

"I know who broke it and how he did it."

"Then you know it was pried off."

"Yes."

"With a good-sized screwdriver."

"Yes."

"And you say Ray Stucky did this at twelve-thirty in the

morning. Having no idea a new lock had been installed. And standing a few feet from your landlady's door. While you were sleeping." Jacob shook his head. He walked over to Ray Stucky and picked something up. "Do you recognize Defense Exhibit Number Two, Miss Barnes?" He returned to show it to her.

"Looks like my screwdriver," she observed.

"The one you used to install the lock."

"I guess."

The judge cleared his throat.

"Yes," she said.

Jacob stared at her a moment. He looked at the screwdriver. He patted its handle into the meat of his palm as if he were considering throwing it into a tree. He faced Ray Stucky, stared at him for some time, then exchanged the screwdriver for a folder. He turned again to the witness.

"Miss Barnes, you have no roommate, is that correct?"

"That's correct."

"There's no one you know, besides yourself, who would have any opportunity to use your phone to call Mr. Stucky."

She tried to catch Mr. Gray's eye but he was too busy, Tex noted, trying to look like a man who knew exactly where this was going. "No one," she said, "including myself."

"And there's no one you know, besides Mr. Stucky, who would try to call you from his residence in Burlington?"

"He tried, but I hung up."

"You hung up."

"Hard."

Jack breathed a small laugh through her nose. Nearly half

the jurors, Tex noticed, shared her amusement—a bad sign his father ignored.

"After March tenth, then, you never spoke with the man you say raped you."

"I did not."

"The man who you say abused and humiliated and degraded you in your own home. You wouldn't be able to stand even to hear this man's voice, much less hold a conversation over the phone."

"Would you?" Lucinda Barnes asked.

"Certainly not," Jacob said, and a wicked thrill buzzed Tex's insides. "All the doors are closed," he whispered.

"Will you shut up?" Jack hissed. She wouldn't look at him, and Tex turned away, her words on his face like spit.

Jacob consulted the folder. "Miss Barnes, do you recall phoning your mother the morning of March twenty-eighth?"

She thought a moment. "It was her birthday."

"And you called her at her home in Waterloo."

"Yes."

"And do you remember who you called immediately after that?"

She picked something from the corner of her mouth, then dropped her hand to her lap. "No."

"Is it possible you called Ray Stucky at his home in Burlington?"

Lucinda Barnes blinked. Judge Tanner watched her.

"I might have," she said. "I don't remember."

Jacob suddenly grew hard of hearing. "I'm sorry?"

"I said I don't remember."

"You don't remember?"

"No." She tugged on an earlobe.

"You don't remember if you called the man you say attacked you?"

She reached for the other ear, but stopped herself. "No. I don't."

"You don't remember if you called the man you say humiliated and degraded you."

"No."

"You don't remember, Miss Barnes, if you called the man you say brutally raped you—"

"Your Honor—" Mr. Gray was on his feet.

"—you don't remember that?"

"Your Honor, the witness has clearly stated her answer!"

"Yes." Judge Tanner nodded. "Move along, Counselor."

Mr. Gray sat down, removed his glasses, and gave the bridge of his nose a pinch. Jacob looked to the jury box as if awaiting signals from a dugout. He turned back to the stand.

"But, Miss Barnes," he said. "Is it *possible* you made that phone call?"

She seemed to shrink a little. Her face was a brittle mask. "It's possible," she said.

Jacob turned away from her. "Your Honor, at this time I'd like to have Defense Exhibit Number Five marked for purposes of identification." He distributed sheets of paper to the judge, the clerk of court, and Mr. Gray, who accepted his with maximum indifference. Finally Jacob showed a copy to Lucinda Barnes and asked if she recognized it. She did. "It's your phone bill," he said, "for the month of March, nineteen seventy-four."

"Yes, it is."

"Which you paid."

"Of course." She glared at him as if he'd just made his most outrageous implication of the day, and the court, Jacob included, had to smile.

"Well then," he continued. "Would you mind telling the jury how many times Ray Stucky's phone number appears after March tenth, the day you say he raped you?"

She studied the sheet.

"They're underlined," Jacob said helpfully. "In red."

"Ten, maybe fifteen—"

"Actually, Miss Barnes, I count twenty-seven times. In the twenty-one days following March tenth you phoned Ray Stucky a total of twenty-seven times. Isn't that correct?"

"Seems so."

"May I take that as a yes?"

She tossed red hair and lifted her chin. "Yes."

Farley Dickerson might have been a great ballplayer, Tex wanted to tell Jack, but he couldn't have hit that grand slam.

He didn't tell her. Didn't even glance her way. He doubted very much if he'd even ride home with her.

"You called him twenty-seven times, Miss Barnes, as surely as you pried that lock off your door."

"That's a lie."

"With your own screwdriver."

"No."

"After you let Ray Stucky in and had consensual sexual intercourse with him."

"I didn't—"

"After he picked up his things and said goodbye at one in the morning."

"No."

"Because you needed a way to convince people that *this* time it was rape. Because you wanted to humiliate and shame Ray Stucky—"

She shook her head.

"—because Ray Stucky was leaving you for another woman."

She opened her mouth to answer, but Jacob turned away, fury in his eyes. "Because in fact," he said to the jury, "Ray Stucky didn't want *in* your apartment, Miss Barnes. Ray Stucky wanted out."

"That's a lie!" she cried. Her mouth trembled and her eyes darted around the room, seeking contact with Mr. Gray, with the jury—with anyone. When she got to Tex, he looked away.

Jacob had heard enough. "No further questions, Your Honor." He returned to his seat and did not look again at the witness, but only sat there, elbows on the table, one hand cupped over a fist, a knuckle to his lips—the way he presided over a chessboard, it occurred to Tex.

Judge Tanner set aside his copy of the phone bill and asked if the prosecution cared to redirect. Mr. Gray declined, then stood to announce that the State wished to rest its case.

"Any more witnesses, Jacob?" the judge asked.

Jacob stirred. "Yes, Your Honor. Raymond Stucky will testify."

The judge nodded and told the jury to recess for five minutes while he and counsel went through a few mundane motions. The jurors rose and began shuffling from their box, and Ray Stucky stood up. He followed the jurors with his eyes, showing his respect, and in the process gave Jack and Tex their first clear view of his profile.

Tex heard a small gasp, and turned. Jack was bumping knees on her way to the doors.

9

"Jack," Tex said, louder than he meant to. Ray Stucky turned, Judge Tanner looked up, the entire courtroom craned as one. Jacob lowered his glasses, frowned, and returned his attention to the bench.

Tex lost ground trying to close the door to District Court A soundlessly, but caught up with Jack just outside the building, where she jerked repeatedly at her bike, trying to extract a handlebar brake from his spokes.

"What is your problem?" he demanded, out of breath.

"Leave me alone." Her bike broke free and she hopped on the seat. She glared at him. "I know that guy."

"What guy?"

"Ray Stucky. I know that creep."

"How?"

She tried to push off and he grabbed her handlebar.

"Let go, Tex, or I swear—"

He held on a moment longer, then released her. "Fine. Go. See if I care."

She glared down the runway of the sidewalk. She took a breath that seemed to calm them both. "One time last summer," she said in a tired voice, "me and Farley stopped in Burlington. Needed some gas and a bulb for the taillight. It was hot, so I got out to watch that Stucky creep change the bulb. Farley filled the tank, then went to the bathroom at the back of the station, and while he was gone, the creep says to me, 'How old're you, darlin'?' I tell him, then I ask him, like I could care less, 'How old're you?' 'Hand me that screw,' he says, 'and I'll tell you.'

"I bend to get the screw," she went on, the red of her face deepening, "and that creep. That jerk—" She squeezed her handle brakes. "He just off and spanks me, right on the seat of my white shorts with his greasy, disgusting hand. Says, 'Too old for teasin', that's how old,' and starts laughing like some kinda pervert demento."

Tex looked down at his bicycle, wanting suddenly to be on it and riding far away from the courthouse. "What'd you do?"

"Called him a creep and threw the screw at his face. I went inside the station and Farley was paying the lady behind the counter and when we turned around he must've seen the handprint on my butt, 'cause he handed me his Coke, walked outside, and positively slugged that Ray Stucky to the ground."

"Farley beat up Ray Stucky?" Tex said, as if he were having a hard time picturing it, though he wasn't.

Jack curled her lip at the courthouse. "My dad don't defend perverts, Tex. He kicks the shit out of 'em."

She pushed off, then, and rode swiftly away. When

he finally recovered his voice, she was well out of earshot, but he hollered anyway, "Dammit, Jack! Even perverts have rights!"

Linda's Mustang sat alone in his father's drive, and Tex went in to find her. He stood still in the kitchen, listening, hearing nothing beyond the slow drip of the faucet. He climbed the stairs soundlessly and peered down the hall toward his father's bedroom and the bathroom. Both doors stood wide open.

In the tub a pool of milky, hair-strewn bathwater burped above the drain, smelling of lilac. He stepped back out, wrestled a moment with better judgment, then eased an eye around the jamb of his father's bedroom door.

Linda lay facedown on the bed, wet hair swept over her profile, two pink insteps nakedly displayed. Her tan legs were exposed, but the rest of her, from mid-thigh to collar and out to the fingertips of her spread-eagle arms, lay beneath the scrim of one of his father's creased white shirts. Her shoulder blades rose and fell quiet as moth wings, and Tex knew that a single step into the room would yield a clear view beneath the canopy of shirttail, up the corridor of thighs and farther, as far as the eye cared to go. But then he thought of Jack, the look of disgust she gave the courthouse, and he turned away.

Back in the kitchen, he grabbed a bottle of Dad's Root Beer and carried it around the corner to the den. He took a seat in the oak swivel chair, propping his feet on the desk the way his father did. The room smelled of old wood and leather, of dusty law, and he sat there a long time, gazing at yellowed depictions of ancient trials hung on the walls—until the clamor of grocery bags in the kitchen startled him and he heard his father call his name. He took a swig of root beer and dropped his feet to the floor. "In here," he answered.

Jacob appeared at the doorway with an apple in his grip. "Thought that was your bike. What are you doing?"

Tex shrugged.

"I see." His father turned to glance up the staircase, listened a moment, then stepped into the room. "Please," he said, "you look so comfortable," and Tex sat back down. "Have you called your mother to tell her you're here?"

"Not yet. But . . ."

"Yes?"

"Can I stay here tonight?"

"Of course." Jacob took a seat on the sofa and began buffing the apple on his knee. He cleared his throat. "That was quite a performance at court today."

Tex knew which one he meant. "I'm sorry." Sudden tears burned in his eyes, threatening to spill.

"I'm glad to hear it. I'm sure Judge Tanner will be—" Jacob leaned forward. "What is it, son?"

Tex shook his head. He couldn't stop thinking about Jack's story about Ray Stucky, or about that cornered, cross-examined Lucinda Barnes. He felt as if he'd seen and heard way too much for one day. He rubbed his eyes hard. "Did you win?"

Jacob stared at the apple. "We got our verdict."

Tex nodded. "Those phone bills did it, huh?"

"They certainly helped."

"How come Mr. Gray didn't have them?"

"He didn't subpoena them. And the witness didn't tell him. In other words, pure luck."

"Pure luck," Tex repeated. It was pure luck that Jack and Farley had stopped at Ray Stucky's station, that Jacob defended Stucky, and that Jack was there to see it. Would his father have taken the case, he wondered, if he'd known what Stucky did to her?

Jacob gave the apple a toss and caught it, the fruit smacking his palm with the sound of a baseball. "And do you know the strangest thing of all?"

Tex did not.

"When I left the courthouse a little while ago, I saw the two of them drive off together in an old green Chevy Impala."

"Ray Stucky and the waitress? What for?"

His father's lips formed a mysterious smile, but he only shrugged and said, "Beats me." He stood to straighten one of the frames on the wall. "I've been practicing law since before you were born, Tex, and few things in all that time have been so repeatedly proven to me as the basic lawlessness of adult relationships."

With that he made his exit and calmly ascended the stairs. Tex thought again of Lucinda Barnes on the stand, scanning the courtroom for a single pair of friendly eyes. Maybe she'd seen Ray Stucky's. Maybe, after all that, she had nowhere else to go.

To get her out of his head, he went to the living room and found the Cubs on TV. He turned the volume loud and wished for a baseball to hold. He wished for Jack's glove over The Hand, for Farley's voice in his ear, and for the pure, inviolable laws of the game.

The next morning, when he arrived at his mother's house, Jack was sitting in the shade of the stoop. Tex dropped the bike and walked toward her, his legs weak from pedaling.

"Tough ride?" she asked.

"Nah. Hot, though."

"Here." She handed him her Coke. They were not in the habit of sharing drinks, and Tex took the gesture as a sign that all was forgiven: Jacob Donleavy could continue in his errant lawyerly ways, but she wasn't going to hold it against his son. He swigged gratefully, not the least bit bothered by the trace of spittle her lips had left on the can. A moment later she ducked into the house, then reappeared with their mitts. She handed him his. "See how that feels."

He flexed the Rawlings open and shut with only the slightest pain. The leather inside felt smooth as skin. "How'd you do it?"

"A new glove is like shoes and women, Tex." She looked him in the eye, deadpan—then gave him a slug. "C'mon," she said.

They resumed their posts down by the Archibald, and though they exchanged tosses in the easy rhythm of teammates, Tex couldn't shake the feeling that some slight damage had been done to their friendship—or whatever it was. As the morning wore on, he kept an eye on his mother's house, looking for Farley to come trundling down the hill and, somehow, repair the damage. Or if not repair it, at least complete, as only he could, their crippled triangle. It was the last chance the three of them would have, Tex guessed, just to throw and catch and joke around, because that afternoon, just after lunch, he would begin his career as a Minnesota Twin.

10

"We're going to a ball game, kiddo," Farley hollered from the kitchen, "not the prom!"

"No kidding?" Tex made a face in the mirror, and continued looking himself over. With its cavernous jersey and drooping, billowy pants, his Little League uniform appeared to have been selected with an eye toward significant future growth. He couldn't have looked more ridiculous, in his opinion, if he were wearing a gown. He took a breath, threw aside the door, and met them in the kitchen.

"Look at you," Caroline said. Her eyes misted and she began digging in a drawer for the Instamatic. Tex braved a glance at Jack; she held two fingers to her lips, manually preventing a smile. Then she dropped the fingers and grew serious. "You look like a ballplayer," she said.

"Right."

"Leastways like a Little League ballplayer. Trust me, Tex, you won't look any goofier than the rest of them."

"Great."

"And anyway you're not finished." She turned to the kitchen table and turned back with his blue Twins cap. She pressed the sides of the bill toward each other, molding it gently, and handed it over. He repeated the ritual and put the cap on. It sat firmly on his head, covered him, shaded his eyes from the hundred-watt bulb overhead, and for the first time he thought he understood why Jack flung herself into the Mississippi to save hers. For a kid like her, or him, or anyone who felt a little bit odd in the world, a good cap hid. A good cap protected.

Caroline found the camera and blinded him with the flash, and they all piled into Farley's VW.

At the Lee County Ballpark, as Farley maneuvered the minibus through cars and gravel dust, Caroline saw something through her window and sighed. "He's here," she said flatly. Tex followed her gaze, saw his father's car, and felt his heart stretch in many directions at once: his father, his mother, Linda Volesky, Farley, and Jack—his entire world—present to watch him take the field for the first time. But as he approached the diamond, he saw that his father sat alone on the lowest level of the bleachers, and was relieved. And disappointed. Maybe Linda had stayed behind for no other reason than to avoid sharing a bench with his mother, but Tex felt slighted.

His father himself presented a second vexation just sitting there. While all around him other parents were decked out in old jerseys and denim, laughing and gesturing with cans of beer, Tex's father sat with one leg crossed neatly over the other, glasses low on his nose, reading the paper. His long white sleeves gave off an embarrassing glare.

Farley nudged Tex in the arm. "That's your old man, there."

"Yep."

"He ever play any ball?"

A tittering from his mother revived Tex's sense of loyalty. "He knows a few things."

"So introduce us," Farley said.

Caroline stopped walking. "Well, okay, you guys do that." She plucked up Willa May. "I'm going over to the, over there, to the concession stand, and get this child something to drink. You coming, Jack?"

Jack began to follow, but Tex grabbed her sleeve. "Jack's coming with us," he said. "She wants to meet a real live lawyer. Don'tcha, Jack?"

She flashed her nastiest smile. "With all my heart."

Jacob rose at their approach. "Hello, son. You're looking very . . . capable."

"You too. This here's Mr. Dickerson. My, uh—"

"Coach," Farley said, extending his hand. "I read about you in the paper this morning. That was some case you had with that waitress."

Jacob nodded and turned to Jack. He shook her hand and said he was pleased to meet her. Jack glanced down and said, "Likewise." Farley consulted his watch, gave Jack a pat on the back, and said, "Why don't you go warm up the rookie, here, darlin'? Game's gonna start in a few minutes."

She was gone before the request was all the way out, but

Tex hesitated. What could Farley possibly want to say to his father in private?

"C'mon, rook," Jack called, and reluctantly he followed.

From the freshly mowed outfield he kept an eye on the two men: Farley had said something and his father appeared to be thinking it over. At last he shrugged, nodded, and did not seem to mind the clap on the back he received when Farley left him for the infield.

"Hustle in, Twins," Farley barked, and all the faces of the boys Tex had been practicing with for the past few weeks suddenly revealed themselves, grinning and spitting from the camouflage of identical blue-and-white uniforms. Wrigley's jersey strained at his belly and Dunsmore's hugged his big shoulders, but for the most part, as Jack had promised, the boys were unified in baggy tailoring.

As his team crowded around him, Farley gave a tug on the bill of Jack's cap. "What's this Redbird doing in our huddle?"

"Spying," she said.

"For the Orioles?"

She shrugged. "They're gonna need all the help they can get."

The Twins laughed and Jack left, collecting a single, sharp slap on the hand from Andrew Ferguson.

Farley hunkered down to remind his boys that even though they were about to play last year's district champs, it was still just a game. They should have fun, he suggested, but if they happened to beat the pants off these bums in the process he'd take them all out to Shakey's Pizza. Tex was wedged between Rummelhart and Dunsmore, and when the

Twins abruptly thrust their hands to the center of the huddle, he had no choice but to shuck off his Rawlings and add The Hand to the pot. Nobody flinched, no hands recoiled. They jerked the human octopus of their arms three times into the air and down again to the tune of "LET'S GO, TWINS!"

Then, the next thing he knew, Tex was standing alone in right field, his heart hammering while his teammates commenced a crickety, melodious chattering meant either to encourage Rummelhart on the mound or to rattle the batter, he wasn't sure which. His parents, he noted, had found seats at opposite ends of the bleachers.

A meeting of wood and ball ended the chatter, and Andrew Ferguson pounced on the grounder, collected himself, turned to first, waited for Jimmy Spinelli, a skinny left-hander they called Spaghetti, to step on the bag—then fired the ball. Spinelli's mitt didn't move except to swallow, and the Twins had their first out of the season.

Fans hooted and Farley called "Attaboy, Frogman!" and the Twins echoed him. Caroline set aside her can of Budweiser to clap, while Jack stuck two fingers in her mouth and reproduced the piercing note of a bottle rocket just before it detonates. For his part, Jacob applauded with perfect urbanity, as if a fine point on a delicate matter had just been made. And so it had. Frog's play, his quickness, his calm, made a fine point to everyone there: it said the Twins had a shot.

The next batter had better luck getting by the Twins' second baseman, a kid whose real name was Burger. The third batter struck out swinging, and the fourth sent a line drive directly into Dunsmore's glove. The district champs were scoreless, and the Twins hustled in to bat.

Farley had scribbled Tex's name low in the lineup, and he retired to the bench with gratitude. Yet he'd hardly sat down before he saw his father do a crazy thing. As Burger grabbed a bat and headed for the plate, Jacob crossed the length of the bleachers, rounded the cyclone fencing, and strolled over to first base.

"Hey, Coach," Dunsmore said. "What's that guy in the tie doing?"

"That's Mr. Donleavy," Farley said. "Your first-base coach. You stop at first base, Big D, you listen to him good. All you guys."

Dunsmore fixed Tex with a grin. "Looks like ballplayers run in your family, Davy."

"Up yours."

He showed Tex his bat. "Know what I'm gonna do when I get in the box? Gonna pretend you're on the mound and smash the first thing he throws me outta the freakin' park."

"You do that."

Burger drove the ball into shallow center, and the Twins were on base. Jacob stepped forward, said something into the boy's ear, and stepped away. Burger assumed a base stealer's posture, no less menacing for his having to keep one foot on the bag. The Oriole pitcher gave him a bored glance, and pitched. Burger sprang, Frog stepped from the box, and the catcher heaved to second, but was late by the length of Burger's fingers.

"Good jump, Hamburger!" Farley called out. "Good wheels! He's another Charlie Hustle, that kid." He gave the thumbs-up to Jacob, who answered with a nod.

Frog waited for a full count, then brought Burger home

with a right-field triple. The Twins' center fielder, a quiet dark-eyed boy named Gomez, lugged his bat to the plate, admired a strike, then popped up to deep center field. Frog held back on Farley's command, waited for the catch, then sprinted home easily.

"Good play, Gomey," Farley called from third base. "Textbook."

Dunsmore gave Tex a wink on his way to the plate.

"Shove it," Tex said. And he did. Over the center fielder's mitt and out of the freakin' park.

The Twins continued to score. Runners shared a few words with Jacob at first base, then a few more with Farley at third, and as the order dwindled steadily toward him, Tex grew increasingly anxious. Spinelli singled to left, and Tex was on deck. Rising from the bench, he tried to locate Jack in the bleachers, hoping for some sort of nod, a smile . . . But she wasn't there. His mother waved, but Tex looked beyond her, searching the grounds, turning all the way around until he spotted that red cap.

She was by the rest rooms. Talking with Frog.

Tex grabbed a bat, a big one, and headed for the on-deck circle. Zimmerman stood at the plate with the patience of a fence post. He got more balls than strikes, finally, and left the box without once swinging his bat.

"That's looking 'em over, Red," Farley said, laughing. Tex took one last practice swing and nearly hit someone behind him. "Whoa!" he heard. It was Frog.

"I'm up," Tex said.

"I know." He tried to hand Tex something, the shriveled skin of some small rodent, it looked like. "It's a batting glove," Frog explained. "It might help you, you know"—he nodded at the skinny end of Tex's bat—"with your grip."

Tex glanced toward the bleachers. Jack was back there, holding Willa May. His father awaited him at first base.

"Thanks anyway," he said, and went to bat.

The first pitch came in low and wide and he swung, so hard and uselessly that the bat nearly whipped around for a second try.

"That's all right, Tex," Farley called. "Good swing, but be patient, now. Make him come to you." The catcher said to his pitcher, "Come right to him, Jonesy, he ain't no hitter." A high fastball came sizzling in and Tex swung again, fouling it into the fencing in front of the Oriole bench. Farley turned to watch the ball roll, scratched his jaw, turned back to Tex. "Okay, Tex. Look one over, now. A walk's as good as a hit."

The third pitch, a curveball, somehow found his bat. A terrible shock erupted in the bones of The Hand, the ball one-hopped out of the infield, and somebody yelled, *"Run!"* Finally he did, but in his panic to reach first base he suffered a black-out on basic concepts and slid feet first into the bag. The play had been at second, and Zimmerman was out. Light applause from the bleachers didn't cover the sound of laughter from the Oriole bench. Even their coach, standing there with his big arms crossed over his chest like a magic genie, was grinning.

Tex dusted himself off. Jacob stepped forward to hand him his cap.

"That was pretty dumb," Tex said.

"Nothing dumb about getting on base, Tex. Now, what's your plan for the next one?"

Tex looked down the long path to second. "Steal?"

"Maybe later. For now, decide what you're going to do when the ball is hit."

With a tug on his cap, Tex forced thoughts of Jack and Frog from his head. "Run if it's on the ground?"

"And if it's in the air?"

"Wait and tag up."

Wrigley came to bat. Took a strike.

"That's a good notion, but you'll lose a lot of ground. If it's caught deep, you'll get to second with a tag-up—but that's all you'll get if it's dropped, too."

Wrigley fouled one over the backstop.

"But if you run halfway to second, Tex, and that ball is dropped, you might get all the way to third and be in position to score."

"And if it's caught?"

"Then you'll still have time to return to first."

"But shouldn't I—"

Wrigley's bat sent his question deep into center field, and Tex was gone. By the time the center fielder regained his feet, located the ball, and heaved it in, Tex was staring at his coach beyond third base. Farley waved him home. Tex ran by him in a dream, left his feet as the catcher knelt to meet the ball, and dropped into the second slide of his career. This time it was necessary—and he was safe.

All the Twins lined up for a piece of The Hand, even Dunsmore. Tex swatted the kid's hand, swatted Frog's, then returned directly to the bench and got off his rubbery, trembling legs.

In the top of the fourth, Tex watched in awe as Gomez

tracked a fly ball on the run, somersaulted with the catch, and came up throwing. Dunsmore ducked the cutoff, and the ball skipped down the base path into Wrigley's mitt, where it remained despite a murderous attempt by the runner to knock it free. The blow left Wrigley on his back, turtled, and sprang Farley from the bench.

"You see that, Ump? Good Christ! Eject this kid before he kills somebody!"

"Ah, sit down, Dickerson!" the magic genie yelled from the Oriole bench.

"Hey," Farley yelled back, "you sit down, Bradley, and take your player—how old are you, kid?"

"Screw you," the kid said.

Farley took a step forward, eyes blazing, and for a moment Tex was sure he was going to slug the boy. But in the next instant something, possibly the terror on the boy's face, made Farley grin. "Yeah, sweetheart," he said. "Go back to your bench. You're out."

"Hey, buddy . . ." A man stood in the bleachers, but Farley turned his back to help Wrigley up from the dust.

"You okay, kiddo?"

"No problem," Wrigley said. "Let's play ball."

"That's the spirit, son."

As the game resumed, Tex looked to the bleachers and got a shock. His father was sitting next to his mother. The last time he'd seen them like that, side by side, was at the 1972 Lee County Elementary Schools Spelling Bee Finals, which he lost to *opprobrium* and a kid named Pervis. A few days later, his father moved out.

A lefty was at bat, and he pounded the ball to Spinelli, who scooped it up and stepped on the bag for the last out of the inning. The Twins held a five-run lead, and Jacob returned to first base. Farley told Wrigley to start warming Tex up; if they scored any more runs, he'd get a shot at the mound.

Dunsmore paused on his way to the plate. "I think you're gonna get that shot, Davy."

"Shove it," Tex told him.

And, taking the first pitch, he did.

Later, Tex would remember jogging out to the mound for the first time in a real game—he'd remember thinking he was going to puke—and he'd remember watching Gomez catch the fly ball that ended the game, but he would not be able to recall a single pitch he'd thrown. He hadn't puked, his left arm was sore, and his team had beat the district champs by eight runs, that's all he knew. It was enough.

Farley couldn't stop grinning and clapping his players on the back. He threw an arm around Jacob and insisted he join them all for pizza.

But no, Jacob was sorry to say, he'd have to take a rain check. He was expected elsewhere.

"*Adiós*, then, Counselor," Caroline said. "Do say hello to your young friend for us." She didn't wait on his reply but bent to take Willa May's hand, turned the girl around, and steered her in the direction of the parking lot—though with the amount of Budweiser his mother had evidently consumed, Tex wondered if Willa May wasn't the one in charge of directions. The sight filled him with equal amounts of shame and devotion, and he was about to go to her, help her along to the car like a good son, when Jack took her sister's free hand, steadying the entire structure, and Tex was left alone with the two men.

Jacob turned to Tex. "You played a fine game, son. Looks like Mr. Dickerson was right about that arm of yours. Can't remember the last time I saw a side-wheeler, but the way you throw, a batter can't tell if the pitch is sinking or rising until it's too late. Kind of like—" He glanced in the direction of Caroline, but didn't finish.

"Two walks, two hits, and *zero* runs, Tex," Farley said. "That's mighty fine relief work."

"Rum did the hard part," he felt obliged to remind them.

"True," Farley said. "But you mopped up like a pro. Won't be long before he's mopping up after you."

Jacob glanced at his watch then, and Farley caught the signal. "See you again Friday, Jacob?"

"I expect so," he said, and as he walked away Tex felt the powerful instinct to join him, to ride in his father's T-bird in the opposite direction of Farley, his mother, Jack, Andrew Ferguson, and the rest of the Twins. Drive back to the big Victorian house and his room and his books, a long night of dinner and talk and the late show with Linda.

But as he began helping Farley bag up the equipment, this impulse became less urgent, and by the time they reached the parking lot it was just one of many low, nearly pleasant aches, like the buzz in The Hand from batting, and the throb in his elbow from throwing strikes he couldn't remember.

11

By the middle of summer, following a compressed sched-ule of two games a week, Tex had fielded five hits, crossed home plate three times, and pitched eight innings with an ERA, Farley calculated, of 4.50. Tex thought this a fine, up-standing statistic—much more impressive than his batting average—until Jack explained earned-run averages and Tex realized what 4.50 really meant: it meant that for every six in-nings he'd pitched, four and one-half kids had crossed home plate.

Farley would brook no discouragement: Tex was doing fine, developing faster than he expected, and anyway, five and one was the best start any team of his had ever had. Farley was so excited by the way the season was going and Tex was so ex-cited by his excitement that neither of them, Tex guessed, would've remembered Jack's birthday if Caroline hadn't done it for them.

But she did, and on a sweaty, airless July night, they

all gathered in the kitchen and cheered like a family when Jack extinguished thirteen candles with a single blow. She opened a small, crayon-scuffed box, took out a gold heart on a chain, and accosted her little sister with a big, loud kiss. The brand-new official Spalding Tex gave her provoked no kisses but made her smile at him in a way he'd never seen her smile before, as if kissing him might not be the most disgusting idea she'd ever had. He looked away, fast, and she moved on, to a tidy package from her grandfather in Florida. The package yielded a ring and a note, which Farley, opening a beer, wished to hear out loud.

Jack skimmed the note and forced it on Caroline.

" 'This ring belonged to your grandmother,' " Caroline read in her best reading voice, " 'to my beautiful Adela. It doesn't fit me worth a darn, so I'm sending it to the prettiest young lady I know. Happy birthday, sweetheart. Wish I could be there. Love, Grandpa.' "

"Oh, that's—" Caroline's eyes shone. "What a beautiful letter."

Jack slipped the ring, a simple band of silver with a dulled green stone, over her knuckle, then pulled it off. "I better keep it someplace safe," she said.

"Safer than your finger?" Farley asked.

"Hush," said Caroline, handing Jack another gift. "This is from your father and me."

It was the kind of box, Tex observed, a kid hated to see under a Christmas tree. Jack opened it and blushed. "Thanks, Caroline. Thanks, Dad."

"We can take it back if you don't like it," Caroline said.

"What is it?" Tex asked.

Jack put the lid back on. "Some clothes."

Farley grabbed another slice of cake. "Well, darlin', aren't you gonna try it on?"

Jack's face was nearing the color of her cap.

"She doesn't have to," Caroline said.

"Sure she does!" Farley gave her a nudge. "Come on, Jack. I wanna see."

Jack glanced at Tex, rolled her eyes, then quietly slipped from the table. After a minute of cake and beer and wine they heard her call from her room, "Caroline?"

Caroline went to the sink and rinsed her fingers. "You boys will excuse me?" When she returned a moment later, Tex thought he could detect, in the fine lines of her eyes, the remnants of a smile.

Then came Jack.

What got Tex first was the absence of the red cap: her hair was combed and very nearly pretty. What got him next was the socks, lacy little green things the color of her eyes. From there he skipped over the chafed and bruised regions of her knees to a breezy white skirt that looked like the game of Twister with just the green circles, shrunk to the size of dimes. At her waist the dress turned stretchy and tight, a kind of polka-dotted Ace bandage that hugged the flat of her stomach, rippled along her rib cage, and swelled, slightly but definitely, with her chest. Tex stared without shame at freckled shoulders, the hollows above her collarbone, but most of all at the tiny golden heart suspended just above the squeeze of fabric, caught in the shallowest of dimples that was, inescapably, her cleavage.

"Wack?" said Willa May.

Farley laughed and stood. "That's her all right. That's my Jackie. My grownup teenage daughter. Holy cow." As he moved to embrace her, Caroline warned him to mind his fingers, and his hug became mostly arm and wrist. Jack responded, it seemed to Tex, with equal restraint. But it was a father-daughter hug, no question, and the first, he realized, he'd seen all summer.

Willa May was put to bed and Caroline made popcorn and the four of them stayed up past midnight, spinning the Life dial with buttery fingers. Tex matched Farley Coke for Budweiser while Jack drove her family of plastic pegs around the game board in a green convertible. She acquired a house, paid off mortgages, sent kids to college, and retired wealthy. Finally, with a self-conscious smoothing of polka dots, she said good night.

"Happy birthday, baby," Caroline said.

"Sleep tight," said Farley, popping open another beer.

In the hallway, navigating separate bedtime rituals, Tex bumped right into her.

"Sorry."

"No problem." She smiled and thanked him, in a hushed voice, for the baseball; she couldn't wait to use it. She tugged at the fabric of the dress and spread her fingers across her stomach. "Think this looks too tight?"

He told her it looked just fine and fled for his room, badly confused by bare shoulders and whispers.

He thrashed around in his bed for over an hour, his anatomy in a vague, stubborn uproar. Finally he lay on his back and returned himself, mentally, to that day after the courthouse when he'd found Linda facedown on the bed. This time he didn't turn away but stepped right up to her insteps, watching as her breathing became a kind of rocking—one shoulder lifting softly, then the other, her hips gently shifting from side to side as if she were some big, exotic fish sidling through shallows. The shirttail began to climb, revealing the tan underside of thighs, climbing toward the point where thighs were no longer thighs, and he knew that if she'd only shift her hips once more the shirttail would slip up, all the way up, and there— But no, she stops, and stretches in her sleep, one painted toenail nicking his knee, a movement that restores the shirt to order, and he is forced to reach down and boldly lift the shirt himself. But then, as he does so, the material rising like mist, she sighs and turns, thigh rolling over thigh, tugging cloth from his fingers in a gauzy fluttering, the cloth all spotted, suddenly, with round green eyes, an infection of green spots, polka dots, and he sees that it's no longer a shirt but a dress, and when she turns all the way over he tries to look away but he can't, caught now by the two green dots of her eyes, and her smile—

And he wanted to stop but was too far gone, the heat in his hand spilling into his guts and his head and his heart, forcing him to turn, to bury his face in his pillow and release a low, horrible moan.

A moment later he rolled back and blinked at the dark. He listened to frogs, feeling ashamed and disgusted.

He thought of Jack's word for Ray Stucky and could not shake it.

Pervert.

Then, through the wall, came the soft spanking noise, and he knew Jack had picked up her glove and was lying over there, face to the ceiling, fielding the ball in the dark.

12

The next morning, shuffling into the kitchen, Tex found Farley and his mother at the table much as he'd left them. The birthday cake was out and they both poked at it with what appeared to be the very last of their strength, while Willa May spun the Life dial around and around. The room was full of too many smells—popcorn and frosting and beer and unchanged diaper and sour, just-out-of-bed adults—and the floor was dotted with too many tiny drops of wine for him to go any farther. He returned to his room and waited for Jack to get up.

When she hadn't stirred by eleven-thirty, he went to her door and knocked. Waited. Peeked in. "Jack?"

A dummy of bedding almost worked, but he knew before he poked it that she was gone. And it wasn't a dummy at all, he discovered, but only the natural disarray of her sheets. Among the tangle he found her nightshirt, a copy of *Sports Illustrated*, one dirty sock, and her mitt, the new Spalding tucked inside. He pulled on the mitt and sat on the edge of her bed, producing the squeak he'd heard many times before, through the wall. What did she think of, he wondered, playing catch in the dark?

He returned to his room, threw on his sneakers and his Twins cap, and snuck out the back door. Jack's bike was gone, but it didn't take long to guess where she'd go on a hot, overhung Sunday in Iowa. He just hoped she hadn't worn the polka dots.

But her Huffy was not among the bikes strewn beneath the Galaxy marquee, it was nowhere on Main Street, and Tex dumped his Schwinn in defeat at Manny's door.

The shop was open, air conditioner running strong. "Haircut?" Manny asked from behind the Sunday *Observer*.

"Just a soda, thanks."

Manny grunted. He was waiting, Tex knew, for the movie to let out so he could stand in his doorway and harangue each boy by name: "Hey you, Billy Ivers, how you see through that mop? Get on in here, boy, before you slam that bike in a tree. And you, Jeff Dunovitz, lookin' more like a girl every day you don't trim that wig."

Tex sat in a chair by Manny's cooler sipping Coke, hoping Jack would pedal by. On the wall above the cooler was a silver plaque engraved with the town's gratitude to Manfred Henry Tate for meritorious acts in the service of the Lee County Volunteer Fire Department. A long time ago, his father had told Tex, Manny saved a small girl from a burning house.

Manny rattled his paper inside out, gave it a shake. "Your friend was here, while ago," he said.

"My friend?"

"Had me going, too—right up till I got that cap off. Ain't nobody held scissors thirty-five years can't tell boy hair from girl."

"Jack was here?"

"If that's her name, then she was here."

"Was she, um . . . alone?"

Manny lowered his paper. "Now, how you think she got a haircut if she was alone?"

"I mean," he stammered, "she wasn't with someone else? She wasn't with another kid—not me, but some other kid?"

"Boy, you hiding some kinda brain damage under that cap?"

Tex met his eyes. "No, sir. I was just wondering."

"Just wondering. You got nothing better to do than sit around here all day just wondering?"

"Yes, sir," he said. "I'm trying to find her."

As Tex approached the mall's glass doors, Jack pushed her way out, backpack straps biting her shoulders. She strode right by him. "What're you doing here?"

"Looking for you," he said.

"Congratulations." She was her old bony self again, red-capped and T-shirted, as if the polka-dot dress had been a kind of trick, a spell from which she'd suddenly, permanently awoken. He shadowed her to the sidewalk. "What's with the backpack, Jack?"

"None of your business." She picked up her bike and swung a leg over the seat.

Tex did the same. "Looks to me like you're leaving town."

She stood on her pedals and began to ride. Tex followed. He waited two blocks, then pulled out his impression of Manny. "Got yourself a fine proper trim, I see."

She ignored him.

"Yessir, jury take one look at that cut they *know* the—"

"I ain't going back, Tex."

He rode up alongside her. "How come?"

She shrugged. "Sick of it."

"Of me?"

"No, Tex, not you."

"Then—"

She braked so abruptly he had to circle back.

"What?" he said, but she just stood there, blinking at the sidewalk. He looked down and saw tears land in starburst shapes almost identical to wine drops on linoleum. The spots vanished as he watched, sucked up by the thirst of concrete.

"It's my mom, isn't it," he said.

Jack sniffed and wiped her face roughly. She looked up with bloodshot eyes. "What?"

He looked away. "My mom's wine. That's why you're leaving."

She stared at him. "Caroline's wine? That what you think?"

"Wouldn't blame you, after your mom and all."

"What about my mom?"

Tex studied the tread of his front tire. "How she died."

"You mean the cancer?"

He looked up. "I thought—"

"You thought what?"

"I thought it was drinking."

"What? Hell's bells, Tex, she didn't *start* drinking till she got cancer. And you would, too. I know *I* would."

His brain seized up in confusion. One of them, Jack or Farley, wasn't telling the truth. Or maybe didn't know it.

She pushed off again and he followed in silence.

"Where you gonna go?" he said at last.

"Florida. See my gramps."

"How much you get for that dress?"

"What dress."

"Manny said you were carrying a box, like a clothing box."

She turned to give him a dirty look, then turned back. "Twenty-five bucks."

"You'll never get to Florida on twenty-five bucks."

"Plus ten from Farley's wallet."

"You stole from Farley's wallet?"

"Tex, I gotta get out of this crummy little town before I go crazy!"

Tex thought suddenly of Andrew Ferguson. Was he part of the crummy little town she needed to escape? He sincerely hoped so.

"Well, you might get to St. Louis on thirty-five bucks," he said.

"Then that's where I'll go."

He didn't want her going anywhere, but if she had to, he guessed it would be better for her to go where she knew some-body, especially a nice old Florida grandfather.

"I'll get you more money."

"How?"

"My dad."

"You can get to his wallet?"

Tex stood on his pedals and took the lead. "I'm gonna *ask* him for it, dingbat."

She took her time catching up to him.

"You are one weird kid, Tex," she said.

They found Jacob on the back porch, sipping iced tea with Linda. A moat of newsprint lay at their feet, requiring Tex and Jack to keep their distance. Linda watched them from her chaise longue, blue eyes peeping over the rim of dark sunglasses. "Well, well," she said. She wore a white knit tennis shirt and a matching skirt poorly designed, Tex noted, for porch lounging. Not to be outdone, his father sat there wearing no tie whatsoever. "Hot day for such a long ride," he observed.

"We were already halfway here," Tex explained, "so we figured, what the heck."

"What the heck," Linda echoed.

Jacob smiled at Jack. "Have the ladies met?"

"Oh," Tex blurted, and made quick introductions. He watched Jack hesitate, then take Linda's hand with a look of wonder, as if she were meeting Lou Brock, and Tex saw something about her he'd never seen before: Jack was impressed by beauty.

Linda seemed equally smitten, holding Jack's hand so long Tex was sure she'd start telling her fortune. "Why don't I get you two something to drink before you both keel over?" she suggested at last, and got up to do it.

Left to himself, Jacob seemed uneasy, as if Linda had taken all sense of repose and humor with her. He sipped tea and refolded his paper, uncrossed his legs and crossed them the other way. The sun seemed to have stuck a fork in the back of his neck.

At last Jack cleared her throat, and Tex piped up. "We came to ask—I mean we'd like to talk. About something."

Jack looked skyward, her thoughts exploding into Tex's skull: *Bad idea, Tex, never shoulda come, you're blowing it already, let's get outta here!*

Jacob adjusted his glasses. "Relax, son. I assume you didn't come all this way to ask the time. Just take a breath, and tell me what's on your mind."

"Jack needs money to go to Florida."

She nearly crumbled beside him. But his father raised an eyebrow, a signal that he wasn't sure he'd heard right but he was willing to hear more.

"Just a loan, Mr. Donleavy," Jack said. "Pay you back soon as I can."

"I will, too," Tex added. "I mean, I'll help."

Jacob removed his glasses, looked for smudges, put them back on. He stood up just as Linda returned with two root beers. "It seems Jack and I have some business to discuss," he told her.

She resettled herself stylishly, impersonating some other kind of lady, Tex thought, one with pounds of dress to cope with and not that skimpy skirt. "Then discuss you must," she said, "as she's come a long way on a hot day."

"You'll excuse us, then?"

She leaned to scoop up the Fashion and Leisure section. "Of course."

Jacob led the way into the house, but at the threshold he suddenly turned, his palm out. "Perhaps, Tex, it would be better if Jack and I spoke alone?"

This was out of the question. Yet the moment Tex began to say so, Jack interrupted. "It's okay, Tex. Be right back."

Tex found the Sports Section and took his father's seat next to Linda. She sipped her tea and poked him in the arm. "I hear you've become quite the ballplayer." He shrugged, keeping an eye on the door to the house. "I'm not much of a fan," she admitted, "but I'd love to come and watch you play someday." She craned forward a little, the better to look at him over sunglasses. "You think that'd be all right?"

He glanced at her and thought of his mother, tried to imagine her sitting in the same bleachers with these knees, this smile. "All right with whom?" he asked.

"What do you mean *with whom*? With *youm*, silly."

He turned away. He shrugged. "Fine by me."

Linda followed his gaze to the shut, unbudging door. "Pretty girl," she said, then returned to the paper.

Tex finished the Sports, Comics, and Farm sections. He drank another root beer, Linda another iced tea. They both got up once to use the bathroom—Tex heard nothing as he passed the closed den door—and still Jack and his father did not come out. Finally, as the day began to cool, as sparrows began venturing from the shade of mulberry bushes, Jacob returned to the porch. He looked exhausted and suddenly, thoroughly old. He held a tumbler of whiskey. He was alone.

"Where's Jack?" Tex asked.

"Asleep on the sofa."

"Asleep . . . ?" Tex thought of the sounds he kept hearing through the wall. Did she have some kind of sleep disorder? His father crossed the porch and stood looking out at the lawn. Linda glanced from Jacob to the open door, then resumed reading. She seemed not to have heard, Tex thought, or simply didn't care, that Jack Dickerson had fallen asleep on his father's sofa.

"Is she sick?" Tex tried at last.

"Hmm?" Jacob almost turned. "No, no. Just . . . tired."

Tex gave his head a shake, as if confusion could be tossed off like drops of sweat. He swatted at a passing green horsefly. "You gonna give her the money?"

"She no longer wants it."

"You talked her out of it?"

"No. I listened, mostly. Until she fell asleep." He appeared to be baffled by something in his drink, and Tex's heart made a strange knock in his chest.

"So . . ." he said, unable to stop himself. "What'd she say?"

Jacob took another swallow of whiskey. "Nothing you don't already know, I'm sure. She misses her mother. Very much. She's clearly fond of Caroline, but it must be difficult adjusting to so much . . . change. I don't know. Perhaps that's why she was running away." He looked to Tex as if he might be able to shed light on the matter, but Tex's mind was scattered all over the place like newspaper.

Jacob raised the tumbler and drained it.

"That's it?" Tex said.

"You expected more?"

"No. She just seemed so . . ." He pressed the heels of his hands into his eyeballs. "She's *asleep*, Dad. On your *sofa*."

Jacob set the tumbler on the railing and turned. "Try to be patient with her, Tex. And also . . ." He sunk his hands in his pockets and began fussing with coins. Tex waited, knowing some kind of great debate was going on up in that lawyer head of his. Points of yellow light, like early fireflies, flared and died in his vision while he waited.

At last Jacob shrugged, and spoke as if it were a trifle. "Just a favor I wanted to ask you."

"Okay," Tex said, though he didn't like the sounds of this at all.

"I thought you might keep your eyes open," Jacob said. "Watch out for her without letting her know it, if you know what I mean."

"Watch out for what?"

"I don't know, exactly. But maybe you will if you keep your eyes open. Do you understand?"

He wanted to say no, he didn't understand, and what's more he didn't care, and wasn't his father taking the mood swings of a thirteen-year-old girl just a little too seriously anyway?

"Can you do that, son?" Jacob asked.

Tex sighed, gave his Twins cap a tug, and said he guessed he could.

Jacob nodded. "Good. Now, kindly go in and call your mother. Tell her where you are and where you've been. If she asks, tell her we've been drinking tea and discussing world issues."

Tex went to make the call feeling like an accomplice to a

plan he didn't get. Worse yet, he seemed to be the only one who didn't get it. How else could Linda sit through all that and say nothing? She understood, he was sure, and she'd been waiting for him to leave, for the moment when she could talk to his father openly, adult to adult, about Jack's case.

He kept one ear tuned to the porch as he talked to his mother, but heard nothing, and when he went back out a moment later he found Linda and his father seated exactly as they'd been when he and Jack arrived. They weren't talking, they weren't even reading. They were just sitting there, staring at the same blue dusk.

13

On their way to the ballpark the next day, Farley pulled into the mall and hit the brakes. "Why're we stopping here?" Tex asked.

"Because," his mother said, gathering up Willa May, "*somebody* has some dress money to spend."

Tex turned to Jack, but she was already at the side door, yanking on the handle. She slid open the door, hopped out, and banged it shut without once meeting his eyes.

"Good luck, baby," Caroline said over her shoulder. "We'll hear all about it at dinner." She slammed her door and the minibus rumbled back into traffic, purged of females.

Farley told him to sit up front but Tex stayed where he was, rocked by poor suspension and facts: Jack was missing a ball game, willingly and apparently eagerly, for the opportunity to go shopping with his mother. His father was right, he decided: something was wrong with that girl.

"Get a move on, slugger," Farley said at the ballpark. "You're dragging that bag like an anchor."

The sight of Linda Volesky in the stands, making good on her threat to come watch him play, only darkened his mood. She wore a skirt of deep, disturbing red, with pleats that spilled from her lap and rippled in the breeze like a crimson manta ray. On her hip hung a small black pouch, not quite a purse, though it was held there by a thin strap looped over the opposite shoulder. The strap itself was a wonder: on its way from hip to shoulder it bisected a plain white T-shirt, dramatizing the landscape of her chest in a manner that drew one kind of look from fathers and sons, another from wives and mothers.

Farley shook Jacob's hand and said, "Howdy, Counselor," with his eyes on Linda. Jacob introduced them. "Pleased to meetcha," Farley said. Linda said, "Likewise," and flashed him a quick, undazzling smile.

"Tell you what, Tex," Farley said, extra-chummy. "I believe it's time you started one."

"You mean—now?" All their eyes were on him, and his heart was pounding. "What about Jack?" he nearly blurted. His first start and she wasn't here!

Farley gave the news to Rummelhart, and Tex went to the mound and began warming up. Wrigley chased down an errant throw, then returned it in person. "Hey, man," he said into his mitt, as if lip-readers lurked everywhere, "that your big sister or what?" Tex glanced at the trio of adults and saw what he meant: from here she did look as if she could be his father's daughter, though there was nothing fatherly about the way both men stood so close to her, and Tex was glad, suddenly, that his mother hadn't come. He wondered if his father hadn't warned her somehow ahead of time. That might explain the pressing need to shop.

"Nah," Tex said. "That's my dad's . . . friend."

"Friend?" came another voice. Dunsmore sauntered up to the mound. "How's your pop get a friend like that?"

Tex sniffed the air. "You smell something, Wrig?"

"Careful, Davy," Dunsmore said, "your little sister ain't here to back you up."

"*Step*sister, moron," he reminded him. "And she's older than I am."

"Oh, yeah?" He looked left, right, and leaned in close. "What's she got under that T-shirt, huh? C'mon, you can tell us."

"You make me sick, you know that?"

Dunsmore shrugged and glanced toward second. "Hey, you don't wanna say, I'll just ask Frog. Hey, Ferguson!"

Frog looked over and Tex stepped toward Dunsmore, a vague plan to remove a chunk of his throat curling his fingers—but just then Farley came jogging out and Dunsmore backed away with a smirk. "We'll talk later," he said.

Farley dropped a hand on Tex's shoulder. "How's she feeling?" Briefly, he thought he meant Jack. "Think you got the stuff?"

Tex rolled the shoulder. Gave a nod.

"Thought so." He turned to Wrigley. "Break him in with fastballs, Wrig. If he's looking good, try out his slider on that big kid with the zits."

He left the two boys standing there blinking at the Reds' bench, where a six-foot kid swung a bat with three weights.

From a distance the kid's face reminded Tex of an old dartboard. "He's big," Wrigley said, and Tex noticed the clean scent of his catcher's breath. Behind them, Frog chewed gum and relayed a throw from Dunsmore over to Spinelli at first.

"What're you chewing?" Tex asked Wrigley.

"What else?"

"Doublemint?"

"Spearmint."

"Got any more?"

Wrigley squeezed two fat fingers into a back pocket, teased free a flattened white pack, handed Tex a stick. He unwrapped the limp thing and popped it in.

"Batter up!" came the cry, and there was nothing left for Tex to do but throw the ball.

The leadoff batter for the Reds turned his first pitch into what would've been, except for the infinite reach of the foul line, a solo homer. He got a piece of the next one, too, but Frog threw him out easily at first. "Way to go, Froggy," Twins called, while at the dark core of his heart Tex wished, even at the expense of his start, that Ferguson had blown the play.

He paid for such thoughts by giving up back-to-back singles, and suddenly the six-footer was at the plate, wagging his bat. Wrigley dangled two fingers, and Tex nodded. If it worked, the ball would come in low and slow, then break to the outside, where Wrigley's mitt would be waiting. He visualized all this as Farley had taught him, checked the runners, stretched, and pitched.

The ball left his fingers on a direct route to the kid's left knee—and never broke. It fouled off bone, and before Tex could even wince the kid was out of the box and limping toward him. Wrigley rushed to cut him off, but the kid shoved him into dirt and limped on. Tex stood his ground, a strange thrill in his guts, as if he'd gotten out of bed that day hoping for nothing more than a public beating.

The kid was on the mound before a fist shot out and landed in the bull's-eye of his dartboard face. He fell quick, like a dropped bat, and didn't move.

"Punk," Dunsmore said, and ballplayers swarmed the infield, pushing and swinging and shrieking. A short fat kid in a Reds cap scratched Tex's neck, and he slapped the kid's rubbery hot face, hard. It felt good.

The other coach and assorted fathers fought their way into the storm, yanked kids apart, sent them spitting and cussing back to the benches. The ump stomped around in clouds of dust. The six-footer moaned, rose to a drunken stance, and was helped to his bench. Play on the other two diamonds slowly resumed.

"In all my damn days!" the ump ranted, kicking dirt like a small, irate bull. "Never have I seen such a bunch of—" he stammered, looking from one bench to the other. "Just completely, totally unacceptable!" He shook his round head.

"Hey," Farley said. "It was an accident. My pitcher's a bit green, but he ain't no hit man." He stood exactly as he'd stood before the fight, chewing the same length of cigar, and Tex realized he hadn't been one of the men pulling boys off each other.

"Accident my ass," the other coach fumed.

"He'd be glad to apologize," someone said, and everyone

turned to look at Jacob. His shirt was half-untucked, his tie askew as if a kid had swung by it. "Provided," he added, "the batter does the same."

The ump stomped over to the Twins' bench. "Who the hell are you?"

Farley grinned and put a hand on Jacob's shoulder. "First-base coach and esteemed attorney-at-law, Jacob Donleavy. Jacob, meet Bill Fogarty."

Reluctantly, Fogarty shook Jacob's hand. Then he turned and pointed at Tex. "You," he said. "Come." Tex followed him to the plate. "All right, Joe," Fogarty called to the other coach. "Send your player, if he can walk."

"I can walk," the kid snarled.

"Prove it," said Fogarty, and as the kid limped over, Tex found himself looking higher and higher, until his neck almost hurt to face him.

"Sorry about the pitch," he said to chin zits.

Thin lips parted on crooked teeth. "No sweat. Part of the game. Sorry I charged you."

Tex shook his tremendous, greasy hand.

"Okay." Fogarty looked up at the kid. "You're outta the ball game. And you"—he poked a finger into Tex's chest—"the only ball you throw the rest of the game had better come from the outfield."

A substitute runner went to first, and Tex gladly traded places with Rummelhart in right field. "Thanks a lot, Donleavy," his teammate grumbled: the bases were loaded with one out.

But they got lucky. The Reds hit into a double play, and the Twins came in, at last, to bat.

Burger struck out swinging, Frog walked, and Gomez advanced him with a grounder through the gap. Dunsmore paused on his way to the plate. "Next time you nail somebody, Davy? Go for the head. That way I won't have to save your ass."

"Shove it," Tex said, and the Twins scored the first two runs of the game.

In the bottom of the third, Tex got to first on a fluke over the shortstop's head. Jacob joined him at the base. "Good hit."

"Lucky."

"No need to be modest, Tex. Not after that humbling display on the mound."

Tex felt the blood rush to his face. "That was an accident."

"Right," the first baseman said.

At the plate, Zimmerman took a strike without blinking, then two balls in a row. Jacob cleared his throat. "I don't see Jack today."

"That's 'cause she's not here." Tex mentally begged Zimmerman not to wait for the walk, to hit the ball and send him to second. The kid took another strike.

"Is anything the matter?" Jacob asked.

"No. Nothing's the matter. She's just a normal weird girl and I could care less."

Zimmerman got his fourth ball, and Tex lit out for second. Wrigley's single advanced him to third base and another conversation.

"That's some cheerleader you got in the stands today," Farley said. "Great set of wheels."

Tex looked to the stands, baffled.

"Legs, Tex. Don't tell me you haven't noticed."

Tex looked away, a dozen secret glimpses of her plastered, like pinups, to the walls of his skull.

"They're okay," he admitted.

Farley laughed. "Guess you're not much of a leg man."

"Guess not," he said, and prayed for Burger to bring him home.

In the bottom of the fifth, Frog took a seat beside Tex on the bench. He looked around, casually, and asked, "Where's your stepsister?"

Tex didn't want to talk about Jack with Andrew Ferguson any more than he wanted to discuss Linda's "wheels" with Farley. Yet, as he glared at his teammate, all jaw muscle and freckles, he found his first real solace of the day: Jack had declined to watch him, Tex, play, but she'd also declined to watch Frog.

"I don't know," he said, a fiendish heat climbing his throat. "I think she went to a movie."

Frog stopped chewing his gum. "Yeah?"

"Yeah."

He looked to the bleachers. "With your mom, huh?"

"My mom? Nah, she's getting her hair done. Jack went off to meet somebody, I guess. Some friend from her school."

Frog nodded and chewed. "She got a name, this friend?"

Tex turned to look him in the eye. "Who said it's a she?"

Frog nodded some more. Shrugged once. Stood. He carried a bat to the plate and struck out swinging.

At dinner that night Caroline pulled a breast from the Colonel's bucket and gave a harrowing account of crowded stores, pushy women, odd sizes, and dressing rooms with doors that wouldn't shut. In short, they'd had a marvelous day of shopping and wasn't Jack dressed to prove it?

She sat there in new Lee bell-bottoms and a big green out-of-season sweater. She poked at her cup of coleslaw and said, "Just trying them on. They're for school."

"For the fall," Caroline explained. "When it's cooler."

Tex looked at the sweater and shuddered with the dread of the coming school year. He would have troubles of his own with The Hand—the usual mixture of fascination and cruelty until his classmates grew as bored with it as with a dissected frog—but he felt sorrier for Jack. Girls would ignore her for being unfashionable, boys for being unspectacular.

"I like the color," he said, just to say something.

Farley sank his teeth into a leg. "You look swell, darlin'."

Later, as Tex washed his hands at the bathroom sink, the door opened and Jack stuck her head in.

"Ever hear of knocking?" he said.

"I knew you weren't peeing."

He bent low and scrubbed hard. "What're you doing, looking through the keyhole?"

"They're called ears, Tex." He felt a sting on his neck and pulled away from her fingertips. "You should clean those scratches," she said. He ignored her. "Man," she said. "The one day I don't go to the ballpark."

"Couldn't have been any more exciting than *the mall*."

"Farley said you could hear the kid's kneecap in Des Moines."

"Ha, ha. What a riot. Now, do you mind?"

"You gonna pee?"

Tex kicked the door shut. Through it she said, "When you're done peeing, come to my room. I got something to show you."

He spent a dry minute staring at his reflection in Ty-D-Bol blue, flushed, and went to her room.

Jack sat on her bed in her old T-shirt and cutoffs, hands tucked between her thighs. Her new clothes lay in a heap near the closet. Tex swept a *Sports Illustrated* from the chair at her desk and sat down. "What?" he said.

Like magic, two cards materialized from her lap. She held them for him to read.

"What are they?"

"Free passes. To a carnival."

"You mean River Days?"

She slumped a little. "How'd you know?"

"Comes here every summer. Some of the rides are good, but most of it's little-kid stuff."

She stood and stepped to her window.

"How'd you get them?"

She shrugged. "At the mall. Put my name in this thinga-majig, and some dork in a clown suit picked it."

Tex glanced at her desktop: Butterfinger wrappers and baseball cards, transistor radio, nickels and pennies, postcards showing pink flamingos and alligators—and also, sprinkled around like seasoning, the tiny blue ticket stubs from the Galaxy Theater. He remembered what he'd told Andrew Ferguson and couldn't believe what a lying little creep he was. And now Jack had two free passes to the River Days Carnival, which at its worst was ten times better than a matinee.

"So, you mean," he said as it dawned on him. "You're inviting me."

"I *was*. But if it's just a buncha kid stuff . . ."

He stared at the back of her neck and wished he had the power to stop everything, to put the world in a freeze-frame just long enough for him to step up and press his lips, very briefly, right there.

"It's not *all* kid stuff," he said at last.

14

The trip to the Lee County 4-H fairgrounds was the longest they'd attempted by bike, and the day was mean: hot and buggy and dense with the fishy humidity of the Mississippi. When their course required them to cross Route 61, Jack spied the diner by the same name and wanted to go in for Cokes. They straddled their bikes on the shoulder, waiting for a chance to cross. Tex didn't know if she remembered who worked at the diner until she spoke again. "Chicken?" she said.

"Of what?"

"Right." She leveled her eyes at him. "Miss Barnes," she mimicked, "do you recognize this boy in the blue Twins cap?"

"What do I care if she recognizes me? I just don't feel like stopping. It's freakin' hot out here and we got another two miles to go, easy."

"Okay, don't have a cow."

"I'm not having a cow," he said, and pedaled out into the violent wake of a semi.

They heard the tinny, amplified notes of the carnival well before they saw the top of the Ferris wheel churning above the trees; and before they saw the entrance to the carnival itself, they smelled cotton candy as if passing through spiderwebs of sugar. They added their bikes to a vast jumble of tires and handlebars and made for the first Sno-Kone cart they saw.

Jack chomped into cherry ice and surveyed the rides. She seemed to have her eye on the bumper cars, but Tex had a notion for speed, for head-whipping, gut-flipping gyrations in a tight, two-man seat. "Octopus?" he ventured. She followed his nod to where giant steel arms dipped and sliced, causing the long hair of girls to tangle in midair like their screams. Tex watched bodies mash together and felt his chest turn warm.

"Cool," Jack said, and they joined the line.

A moment later Tex felt a tap on his arm. "You guys in line?" He turned to find a kid standing there, about his age, with black, neglected hair leaking out from under a black Pirates cap. The kid smiled at Jack, revealing a nugget of silver where one of his front teeth used to be. "Mind if we cut in?" The kid gestured to the three boys behind him, also in Pirates caps, grinning and elbowing one another. To the rear the line extended itself by several kids and a few adults—hardly worth cutting into, Tex thought. He looked to Jack, but she only shrugged and turned back to the Octopus.

"C'mon," the kid said to him. "Be a bud."

He was about to relent when a little girl gave the kid a push and said, *"No cuts."* Two long braids hung from her head like ropes, like reins somebody had let go of.

"Aw, shut up," Silver Tooth said.

"I don't have to, and if you don't *move*"—she pushed again—"I'm gonna tell my dad."

"Yeah? Where's he?"

Beyond the little girl, a few kids back, a man raised his hand. It was a big hand, attached to an arm that looked capable of denting the bell on the Strong Man Scale.

The kid swallowed silver and said, "Hey, that's cool." He glanced at the back of Jack's Cardinals cap, observed the length of her. "Catch you later," he said to Tex, then turned and knocked through his buddies like a bowling ball through pins. The buddies punched one another, cussed, and followed.

"You know those guys?" Tex asked Jack.

She gave the effect of looking over her shoulder. "Who, those guys?" She shook her head. The line began to move. "I mean, I might've played ball with them once."

The ride wasn't what Tex expected. It wrung them violently and made his stomach surge but failed to squeeze a single scream from Jack, and when it flung them together, one way, then the other, she felt as stiff as the bar across their laps.

Afterward, despite his assurances that it was pure kid stuff, she insisted on taking a car through the Devil's Playground. It was dark in the playground and they sat close, but she was not sufficiently threatened by any of the Devil's tricks to lean against him or grab his arm. "How 'bout the Crazy Cups?" he suggested, back in daylight. Sometimes the ride would stop and you'd find yourself alone at the back of the carnival, facing the river, quietly rocking.

"Okay," Jack said, "but first I gotta pee." He pointed her

in the direction of the Porta-Johns and told her to meet him by the Crazy Cups when she was done.

On his way to the ride he saw several black caps heading his way and wanted to turn around, but it was too late. He jammed The Hand in his pocket and met their surly faces head-on.

"Hey," the kid with the silver tooth said. "Where's your friend?"

Tex shrugged. "She's around."

"She ditch you?"

Tex made a contemptuous noise. "She's using the john, if it's any business of yours."

The kid showed his palms. "Hey, man. Just trying to be friendly." He glanced at Tex's cap. "You play for the Twins? Me and the boys here are Pirates. We were thinking maybe you and your friend might wanna join us for some Buds we got stashed."

Tex blinked at him. "Buds?"

Another kid stepped forward. "*Buds*, man. As in the beer that made Bud wiser? Man, this guy ain't cool."

"Probably a narc," another kid snarled.

"Shut up, morons," Silver Tooth said. He smiled at Tex. "So? Whaddaya say?"

Tex turned, but saw no sign of Jack. He turned back with a shrug. "Where you gonna be? Maybe we can meet you."

"Ferris wheel? Ten minutes?"

"Ten minutes. Okay."

"Cool." He turned to his boys. "Move it, retards."

Five minutes later Jack still had not returned, and Tex began to pace. He walked all the way back to the Porta-Johns and watched plastic blue doors open and shut for ten minutes, then walked away. A thought began to expand in his skull like helium in a balloon: she *had* ditched him. He toured the perimeter of the carnival, and when he could think of nothing else to do, he went to the Ferris wheel. The Pirates were nowhere in sight.

"Take a ride?" asked an old man in coveralls. He held a giant red lever in his knuckly, sun-baked fist.

"A ride?" Tex said.

"Biggest wheel in the state of Iowa. Hell, you can see *Nebraska* from the top of this baby."

Tex showed him his pass and he stopped the wheel.

"There you go, fellas."

A little boy tried to climb in with him, but Tex held out his hand. "I want to ride alone."

"Sorry, buck," the old man said. "Nobody rides alone so long's there's somebody else waiting. Besides, this here tyke's too small to fly solo." The boy looked up at Tex, tufts of cotton candy clinging to his face Fu Manchu style. The old man locked them in.

They rose and dropped again five times, the boy screaming the whole way like the volunteer fire alarm, and no sign of Jack's red cap anywhere. When the old man finally let them off, a man and a woman were waiting. The boy ran to his mother while the father pinned Tex with dark, narrow eyes.

"Don't look at me, mister," Tex said in passing. "I didn't wanna ride with your bratty kid."

He'd begun to make his way to the carnival entrance, to see if her bike was still there, when a barker called out,

"There's the kid with the golden arm!" The barker grinned at him, gesturing with a baseball. His head had been shaved with a dull machete. Tex stopped, his first mistake.

"Attaboy, you got the arm, I knew it the second I laid my eye on ya." He leaned forward, indicating the lusterless, milky glaze of his left eye.

"You don't know me," Tex said.

"Course I do. You're the one's finally gonna win that big red rabbit back there, the one every little sweetheart's had her sweet blue eyes on all day long, the one not a one of these sorry excuses for boyfriends could win, but you will, and I know it. Be glad to be rid of the thing, tell you the truth, so big and red sitting back there, makes me kinda nervous, know what I mean? So here you go, here's a ball, first one's free to the kid with the golden arm."

Tex gripped the ball and the barker mimed a batter at the plate, then stood aside, laughing insanely.

"Go ahead, man," somebody said.

It was Silver Tooth. He and his boys stood huddled between the milk bottle booth and the target shoot. They all looked about as antsy as frogs trying to cross a highway. One of them was missing.

"You guys in line?" He stepped back, offering the ball.

"Not for this, man. Go ahead. I hear you got some stuff."

"Where'd you hear that?"

"You throw for the Twins, right?"

"Yeah."

"Ah *ha*!" cried the barker. "The eye don't lie! Pill-slinger written all over him!"

"So they say you got some stuff." The kid flashed that silver cap and Tex couldn't decide if he liked him or hated him. He was full of crap—no doubt about that—and yet Tex found that he liked the idea of a kid he'd never even seen before knowing about his "stuff."

He pulled out The Hand and faced the milk bottles. The trick was not in knocking them down, he knew, but in getting them all off the barrel. He took a breath, pictured the center of Wrigley's mitt, and threw. Bottles went flying.

"Nice throw, man," Silver Tooth said.

"Did I tell ya? Did I?" The barker harassed bystanders with his crazy dead eye. "That arm is pure Hall of Fame, folks. Vida Blue, look out!"

Tex smiled and looked around for Jack. Maybe she'd like the red rabbit.

The barker handed him a tiny polka-dot elephant in a cellophane wrap. "Here you go, kid."

"Hey," Tex said. "You said the red rabbit." He pointed to the huddle of boys. "I got witnesses."

"You did, man," Silver Tooth confirmed. "The kid gets the pink bunny."

Blood rushed to his face, but Tex kept his eyes on the barker, who stood there grinning like a rabid dog. "You boys are right smart to remind me, but allow me to direct your attention to the Official Rules of the Game, as posted right here in plain black-and-white." He read from a painted square of plywood: " 'Knock all three bottles from the barrel and win a prize. Win three prizes consecutively and take home the Deluxe Grand Prize. Award of prizes is based solely upon the judgment and discretion of Carnival Employees.' That's yours truly, boys, and I'm just as happy as a lapdog to offer your southpaw chum here a chance to prove it weren't just luck hopped those bottles down from that barrel, as he and I both knows it weren't." He presented another ball. Tex reached for it, but the lunatic pulled it away. "Whoop. Didn't you hear me? *First* one's free. Fitty cent thereafter."

Tex was ready to walk away when the missing kid emerged from between the tents. He turned red at the sight of Tex, pounded another kid on the arm, and said, "You're up." The other kid rubbed his arm and disappeared behind canvas.

Silver Tooth pulled coins from his pockets and dropped a handful into the barker's palm. "Two more tries for Lefty, here."

"That's the spirit." The barker offered the ball again.

Tex looked at Silver Tooth and his mysterious, nervous crew, then at the barker, then at the ridiculous stuffed elephant in his hand. If Jack were here, she'd say, "To hell with the elephant, Tex. Go for rabbit."

He grabbed the ball, took a step back, and repeated his first throw—an off-center fastball that left the top of the barrel clean.

"Hey, kid," the barker said. "Damn. That's good throwin'." He dug a fingernail into his face, as if his wrinkles were grooves he'd carved there himself. "Now you got two elephants. A good-looking pair, if you ask me." He began restacking milk bottles. "Any girlfriend would be proud, proud. Ain't that so, fellas?"

Silver Tooth and the others agreed it was so, no question.

"Gimme another ball," Tex said.

"You sure?"

"It's paid for." Tex held out his hand, and the barker fished a fresh ball from his apron, held it to the light, flipped it to him. "That there's my special A-one Good Luck Ball. Catfish Hunter give it to me personally." The ball was lopsided and underweight. Tex gave the barker a grin and cleared the barrel.

The barker stared at him, wet his lower lip with his pointy tongue, then turned to the crowd. "Eureka, folks! We got a winner, here! Yes, sir, look how easy it is to knock three milk bottles off a barrel, so durn easy even a runty little kid can do it. Step right up and you, too, can take home one of these fabulous giant stuffed creatures!"

While the barker worked to pull down the rabbit, Tex turned to thank Silver Tooth for the throws. But he was gone. The other kid was back, now, and the three remaining members of Silver Tooth's gang looked lost and pathetic without their leader. They pushed halfheartedly at each other and cussed incoherently.

"Where'd the other guy go?" Tex asked.

"What other guy?"

"The kid with the—" He was behind the tent, Tex suddenly knew. He *had* been waiting in line, they all had. Not to throw baseballs or shoot guns, but for some secret show going on back there. And Tex was somehow part of that show. The sideshow, maybe. The freak. His heart began pounding.

"Move it, retards."

The boys stepped aside, and Tex entered the dark alley between the tents, the sound of his own breath in his ears like crashing milk bottles. Walls of canvas narrowed with each step, squeezing out daylight and filling his nostrils with chilled, moldy air. He tripped over something, a stake in the ground, and continued on until suddenly he was standing in another tent, some kind of dim, reeking storage tent, and there was Silver Tooth, sitting on a rolled-up log of canvas, a can of Budweiser in one hand. And there was Jack.

"Jack," Tex said, and she jumped to her feet, leaving Silver Tooth's hand hanging there, caught in midair, as if she were still sitting beside him. As if his hand were still up under her shirt.

Tex's feet took him slowly back down the canvas alley, into carnival noise and sunlight and Pirates. As he passed the barker, he heard him call, as if from the bottom of a scummy swimming pool, "Hey, kid! Kid! Don'tcha want yer pink bunny?"

Boys were down there with the barker, all of them laughing like devils.

15

Tex must've thrown thousands of baseballs that summer. He threw so many he dreamed of them at night and woke up with the feel of their stitches on his fingertips. He threw so many he knew when one was regulation and when one was not just by touch. In truth, he hadn't thrown thousands of baseballs but a few dozen baseballs hundreds of times each. Baseballs were not like stones heaved into a river. Baseballs almost always came back.

Stones, never. He dug one from the sand and rubbed it clean. The bank was thick with them, cut from mountains and shaped by current and dropped along the way like Easter eggs, so smooth and perfect you had to pick them up—and when you did, when you held one in your hand, even if you'd never touched one your whole life, you knew exactly what to do with it. The shape of it *told* you.

He cocked his arm and flung the stone hard. It skipped along the skin of the river five times, disappeared on the sixth. A good life for a stone, he thought.

"Nice one," he heard, behind him. He didn't need to look. He only wished he'd gone someplace else. Someplace she'd never been before.

He went about his business, showing her how little he cared that she'd found him. How little he cared about anything she did—least of all with boys like Andrew Ferguson and Silver Tooth. She was just a dumb, skinny girl who happened to be his stepsister.

She came forward. "I guess you think you saw something back there. Some kinda big deal."

He dug up a fresh stone. "Not really."

"Then why'd you ditch me?"

He flung the stone, but it sank without a single skip. "Didn't feel like waiting in line."

"For what? Brains? You should've hung in there."

"You don't need brains to not give a crap."

Jack sighed, and said nothing. Then, "I don't care if you give a crap, Tex. I just wish you'd listen, just for a second, and then you can think whatever you want."

He bent to free another stone from the bank.

"But I guess you'd rather throw rocks at the water."

He flipped the stone, a reject, into the water. Jammed his hands into his pockets. "I'm listening."

Jack stood beside him, toeing the sand with her sneaker. "Last year, at school, I was the new kid, right? The new weirdo girl with short hair and a hick accent. All the girls hated me. Or anyway they ignored me. When I started playing ball with the boys, *then* they hated me."

"You just walked right up and started playing ball," Tex said.

"No. For a long time I stood around watching, knowing I could hit and throw better than the pack of them, and I guess they sort of caught on, because they finally got around to saying I could play, but I had to do something first."

Tex stared at the river and remembered the day it caught them both in its current. He wondered what it was like at the bottom, down there with the stones, in the dark, unable to hear a thing.

"They'd let me play as long as I did some things."

He didn't want to ask. But he had to. "Such as?"

"Such as totally dumb stuff. Like what you saw back there."

He thought a moment. "Those guys didn't exactly look like they were playing ball, Jack."

She was suddenly sitting, as if the bank had shifted radically beneath her. She crossed her legs and sank her fingers into silt. "Those were the boys, Tex. From school. They were following us around, and when I came out of the john, that creep Alan Michaels, with the silver tooth? He came up and said if I didn't go back there with them he'd tell you all about me and all the stuff I did, which probably would've been mostly his ugly mouth telling a buncha filthy lies." She took a deep breath, then fell silent.

A strange fatigue spread through Tex's legs, and he joined her down on the bank. Like old times.

"And you think I would've believed him," he said.

She squeezed a clod of wet sand and flung it, but it came apart in midair, peppering the water. "All I know is you'd have seen me different."

Tex stared at the river and knew she was right: she'd begun the summer a wiry, hotheaded little bully, she'd surprised him with breasts, and now as they sat there in separate funks, he couldn't stop thinking of that kid's hand up under her shirt, the lazy grin on his face, as if breasts, like baseballs and stones, were meant for the hands of boys.

And maybe they were. Maybe guys like Alan Michaels and Joey Dunsmore—maybe even Andrew Ferguson—had already figured this out: if you wanted to touch, all you had to do was reach.

Jack stiffened but made no attempt to stop him, and Tex watched The Hand cross the space between them and settle, like some hideous, flying squid, on her breast.

It was soft and warm through her shirt, bigger than Tex expected. A pliant little tip rubbed, like a pencil eraser, the scars of his palm.

When he finally did look up, Jack was looking right at him, though she might as well have been looking at a tree, he thought, or a rock.

"Big deal, right?" she said.

He kept The Hand on her breast a moment longer, then removed it, and for a long time they just sat there, hip to hip, watching the river.

16

Monday came at last, and Jack and Caroline conde-
scended to return to the ballpark. The minute they all reached
the bleachers, Jack made a break for the outfield to join the
warm-up already in progress, and Tex let her go, glad to put
distance between her complete, knobby self and the memory
of that soft, heated detail of her, that *big deal* that resided now,
like his scars, in the palm of The Hand.

Jacob cleared his throat and offered to get the afternoon's
first drinks, and Caroline said it was a marvelous, imperative
plan. Her smile made Tex notice that Linda was not there.

He went along to get the drinks, convinced now that his
father was running some kind of interference between the two
women, making sure they never crossed paths in his presence.
Having no reason to believe his father wouldn't admit to such
an essentially humane scheme, Tex sprang his theory.

"Ridiculous," Jacob said. "Where would you get such a
notion?" Almost as quickly he put his hand on the back of

Tex's neck and gave a squeeze. "Not that your premise is ridiculous, Tex. I'd do almost anything to keep your mother from having to spend an afternoon in the company of Miss Volesky, particularly when the young lady decides to . . ." He removed his hand from Tex's neck to scratch the back of his own. "When she chooses to appear especially . . ."

It was a rare treat, seeing his father struggle with the English language. Tex couldn't resist helping out.

"Sexy?"

Jacob turned, eyebrows high, and nearly collided with the concession booth. With some difficulty he located his wallet, and somebody's plump, cheerful mother handed over the Budweisers.

"I was going to say free-spirited," he resumed on the way back. "But what's the difference?" They walked along, mulling this one over until Jacob said, in a less speculative tone, "I would never presume to suggest to your mother or Miss Volesky when and when not to attend a baseball game, Tex. They are grown women. And these days, as you might have noticed, grown women do pretty much anything they please." He didn't wait for the bleachers, but popped one of the Budweisers and took a belt Farley would've admired.

"So then . . ." Tex began.

"Yes?"

"Where is she?"

"Who, Linda?"

Tex nodded, and when Jacob spoke his voice was weary. "Like I said, Tex. She's a grown woman."

———

To Tex's amazement, Farley gave him the start. Tex worried briefly about hitting another batter in the kneecap, worried briefly about losing the game. But mostly, as he slung the ball toward Wrigley's mitt, he found a baseball was just a big round stone, and that throwing it where you wanted was the easiest thing in the world.

He found that Silver Tooth was right: he had *stuff*.

He made it to the middle of the fourth, runless, before Farley came out to relieve him.

"Let's save some of that for tomorrow, whaddaya say?"

Tex had never seen his stepfather look so proud. *If only you knew*, he thought, recalling the riverbank.

After the win, Farley made the Twins sit down and shut up.

"I guess you know where this win puts us." He stared them down like a surgeon with very bad news. "That's right," he said, "*alone*, at the top of the district. We beat the Pirates tomorrow and we're a lock for the pennant. And how do we beat the Pirates? By playing the game we've been playing and not losing our heads. Keep our heads, and we'll get a shot at the Regionals, and after that—the *Series*, boys. All we gotta do is remember one simple concept."

The same clueless glance hopped from one boy to the next. A crow flapped overhead.

"Nobody on God's green ballpark can beat us," Farley said, "except us." He gave them a final looking over, then grinned like a madman and thrust his hand to the center of the huddle. Twins tossed hands into the pot and, finally, so did Tex.

Farley wanted to take everybody out for pizza, but Caroline stepped forward to remind him for the second time that day about the Pre-School Party. This was not a party for preschoolers, as it sounded, but an annual event staged by the Lee County Superintendent of Schools, an opportunity for area educators to come together in an informal setting a month before the first day of classes to exchange philosophies on the shaping of young minds and to drink like fish.

Back at home, Farley got a head start, grumbling from kitchen to bathroom to bedroom with a can of beer welded to his hand. Caroline clacked into the kitchen on heels and asked Jack to fasten the clasp of her necklace, a job Tex was not too disappointed to lose.

"You look nice, Caroline."

She touched Jack's face. "Thanks, baby." She clacked away, then clacked back, a fancy little purse in hand. She gave them the lowdown on the tuna casserole in the oven and showed them for the fourth time where she'd posted the superintendent's number, just in case.

"They're not morons, Caroline," Farley said.

Tex and Jack exchanged a glance.

"Thank you for your input. Can I at least tell them when we'll be back?"

"I'll tell them." Farley guided her toward the door. He winked at Tex. "As soon as humanly possible."

An hour later Tex and Jack sat down to dinner. He watched her wash down a single noodle with a sip of milk and knew she was thinking hard about something, and was afraid he knew what. The thick, fishy steam of the casserole put him in mind of the riverbank, The Hand rising, drifting, landing—

"What're you looking at?" Green eyes came stabbing through the steam, and he knew he'd been staring at her.

He dipped his head and began stuffing casserole into his mouth.

"Have you lost your mind, Caroline?"

"Just tell me I'm wrong. Look me in the eye and say, 'You are wrong, Caroline.' "

Farley and his mother were home from the Pre-School Party, and Tex was no longer asleep. Moonlight spilled into his room like a searchlight.

"I'll look you in the eye and say you maybe shouldn't have drunk so much." From the sound of it, they were in the kitchen, their voices bouncing off the hard floor.

"You beer-swilling hypocrite," his mother said. "I wish you could've seen yourself, slobbering down that girl's blouse. Tex's own teacher, for God's sake."

It took Tex a moment to realize that the "girl" she was talking about was Ms. Riley—serious, pretty, modern Ms. Riley.

Farley snorted. "Now I *know* you're drunk," he said, and Tex was seized by the urge to rush out there and tell the fat slob to leave her alone, go back to Arizona, get bit by a rattlesnake. But he didn't budge, and in a moment Farley said, more gently, "Aw, c'mon, Caroline."

"Hands off, pig."

Heels struck linoleum, then carpet, then linoleum again in the bathroom, where Tex heard her shut the door and lock it. In a moment the toilet flushed, the bathroom door creaked open, and their bedroom door banged shut. Now it was Farley's turn to use the bathroom, and the sound of it, like a garden hose held high over a bucket, was almost too loud to bear. He took so long Tex was sure the bowl couldn't hold it all. Finally he flushed, the bedroom door opened, clicked shut—and that was the last Tex heard.

He took a breath and stared at the ceiling. He was ready, all at once, for summer to end. He'd had enough of baseball and Jack and Farley and this crazy house. He wanted to get back to the safety of school, of reading his books and being excluded, of coming home to his father's big empty house.

A knock on the door startled him, jerked him upright in his bed. He stared at the seam of light beneath the door where the hallway night-light crept through. But no feet obstructed the light, nothing stirred, and he decided he must've dozed off, must've dreamed it. No one had knocked.

Then he heard it again. But not from the door—from the wall. He sent back a soft, two-beat rap. She answered with the same two beats, then added another short burst. Tex composed a highly complex series of knocks and sat back to await her reply. Nothing came, and finally he sent her a one-note question—*Jack?*—but she'd either quit the game or gone to sleep.

"As if I cared," he said, hoping she heard it. He turned away, slugged his pillow, and forced his eyes shut.

He couldn't have counted to three before she knocked again. He flipped back to the wall and rapped once, hard.

Nothing.

He tried again. She didn't respond, and he threw aside the sheet, stepped into the lower half of his Twins uniform, and stomped out of his room. Barged right into hers.

"What do you think you're doing?" she hissed. The whites of her eyes were blue in the moonlight.

"What do I think *I'm* doing?"

"Shut the door, will ya? *Quietly.*"

He shut it as quietly as a dropped cotton ball, and stepped up to her bed. "Why the heck—"

"Shh!"

Tex glanced toward Willa May's crib in the corner, but he could tell by the sound of her breathing that he didn't have to worry about waking that kid up. "Why're you knocking on my wall?" he demanded in a whisper.

"To see if you're awake."

"Brilliant, Jack." He glared at her. She lay with her arms at her sides, her nightshirt stretched across her bones like Saran wrap. She scooted a little toward the wall.

"Might as well have a seat, long as you're here. Only for a second, though. Wouldn't want somebody catching us like this."

He hesitated, then perched himself on the extreme edge of her mattress. The air seemed too warm, as if a vent were pouring out heat from under the bed.

"Like what," he said.

She rolled her eyes. "Like whaddaya think?"

He stared at the glass cardinal hanging in her window, glowing with moonlight. "I don't know what to think," he said. "About anything."

She raised her arms and put her hands behind her head, a movement he knew must've hitched up the nightshirt some. Miles off, near the center of town, the volunteer fire alarm began a lazy keening, rising and falling like a giant's wheezing.

They listened until it stopped, replaced now by the distant answer of sirens.

"Maybe you think too much," she said.

"And you don't? You don't think about things?" He turned and got an eyeful of bare knees. He'd seen these knees a hundred times, yet now, here, the sight of them sent hot needles into his chest. "You saying you don't think about, for instance . . . by the river?"

"You're pretty freaked out by that, huh?"

"You're not?"

She shrugged. "Not particularly."

He dug fingernails into the palm of The Hand. "What about before?"

"Before what?"

"Before, at the carnival."

She sighed. "That was like I told you, Tex. Didn't even feel it."

"Bet they did."

She eyed him in the blue light. "You jealous, Tex?" She smiled, and he kicked a T-shirt in the direction of her closet.

"Not of those losers. But . . ."

"But what."

"What if somebody else wanted to, you know—"

"Grab my boobs?" The bed creaked as she rose to her elbows. "It would depend."

"On what?"

"On whether or not I liked him, of course."

Tex looked up to the hazy figure of Lou Brock on the wall. Stealing second.

"It wouldn't depend on me, then."

She sat up to stare at him from close range. "Are you saying I shouldn't let anybody but you touch my boobs?"

"No! I didn't—I wasn't—"

"You *are* jealous." She fell back on the bed with a giggle.

Tex wanted to get up, march out, and slam the door behind him, but he couldn't imagine what he'd ever say to her again after that, so he took a breath and asked, with all the indifference he could muster, "What about Frog?"

"What about him?"

"Would you let him? Have you?"

She didn't have time to answer. A creak in the hallway gripped both their throats, and Tex felt his heart leap at the sight of two dark patches, like eyes, shifting in the light beneath her door.

17

"Wait—" Jack said. She tried to grab his arm, but Tex was too quick—across the room and into her closet in an instant, ducking hangers, crouching, pulling the door behind him. But it wouldn't shut and he had no time to remove the T-shirt blocking the way before Jack's door opened and a silhouette filled the frame. Tex couldn't let go of the closet doorknob without the door springing back open, so he froze, a wobbly gargoyle, The Hand gripping the knob, his heart pounding like fists inside his chest. The glow from the hall night-light slipped past the silhouette and fell like snow over Jack's bed, highlighting toes, kneecaps, pulled-down nightshirt, and an expression of sleep so convincing, Tex saw, she might've just died.

In another second the light lifted off her and her door clicked shut and the room was restored to darkness. The pounding subsided in his chest, and Tex remembered to breathe. He wondered at his panic, his fugitive reflexes, the paralyzing fear of being caught. At *what*, he didn't know; he was twelve.

He'd begun to stand, the first step in the direct course that would return him to his bed, when he heard a noise. He held his gargoyle crouch and listened: it was the sound of breathing. And not the breathing of a girl—not even two girls. It was the deep, gusty breathing of a large man flat on his back with a gut full of beer.

Only he wasn't on his back, Tex saw as his eyes adjusted. He was leaning against Jack's door, a fat specter in the moonlight, a jumbo ghost in boxer shorts.

Then the specter belched and Tex almost laughed out loud.

He was still drunk, and Tex was safe. Any second now he'd realize his mistake, give a salute, and leave. *Sorry, sports fans!*

When this didn't happen, Tex looked to Jack. She hadn't moved, and her eyelids wouldn't twitch, he knew, if you bent down and blew on them. He admired her control even as it gave him, for some reason, the creeps.

Farley peeled himself from the door and began a slow lumber across the room, his big feet mashing clothes and sticking to the covers of baseball magazines. A Spalding scooted toward Tex fast and knocked once, hard, at the base of the door; the impact buzzed The Hand and trembled down his spine. Jack didn't move.

Farley left his view, but the shadow across Jack's bed told him he now stood in front of the window, near her desk. He heard a soft scraping of metal on wood, then the splash of baseball cards hitting the floor; Farley had picked something up. "Ah, darlin'," he murmured. "I'm feeling low-down and lonely." He set it back down, and Tex knew from the glassy thunk that he'd been looking at the framed photograph, or what he could see of it in this light.

Still Jack didn't open her eyes, not even when Farley stepped up to the edge of her bed and hovered there, slump-shouldered, obstructing her nightshirt from Tex's view and giving her, now, the illusion of wearing nothing at all. It was an illusion he wished would pass more quickly than it did, as it reminded him that he was sitting in a place he shouldn't be, watching something he had no business watching—which, he still supposed, was nothing more than the clumsy grieving of a onetime minor leaguer, his stepfather, a basically decent man with no more flaws than the next, the coach who'd made him into a ballplayer and who, he now and then believed, loved him like a son.

Farley sat down on the edge of Jack's mattress, pinching from it a complaint Tex knew well. He sat exactly where Tex had sat a few minutes earlier, but facing the other way, as if he thought Jack's toes were her face. Her face itself was now obscured, so Tex was surprised when he heard her say, "You're just tired, Daddy. You should go back to bed."

He'd never heard her call her father that before. Yet more startling than the word was her voice, which, though whispered, was the voice of a grown woman trying to comfort a child.

"You and your sister are all I got in the world," Farley said, suddenly sober. "You know that, don't you?"

"You got Caroline," Jack corrected him. "And Tex."

The sound of his own name made Tex flinch.

Farley stared at her feet and shook his head. "You're my best girl. My sweetest sweetheart. Don't know what I'd do without you. I'd be lost."

"I'm not going anywhere, Daddy," she whispered.

"You're everything and I love you. You know that, don't you?"

"I know, Daddy. But—"

A big hand floated out and landed, fluttering, on her right foot. "You know I'd never do anything to hurt you. Don't you?"

"Yes, but—"

"Shh, darlin'. Hush, now. Daddy just wants to sit here a minute beside his best girl, his only girl . . ." His hand slipped down the slope of her foot, to her skinny white ankle, where it stopped and gripped. A tide of cold fluid rushed upward through Tex's knees, through his groin, and into his guts. He felt himself listing, capsizing with the weight of it. He blinked and held tight to the doorknob, squeezed it as if it were also Jack's ankle and he wished to hurt her enough to wake her, to wake all of them, from this dream.

Don't do it, he silently pleaded. *Please, Farley. Coach Dickerson—*

But they dreamed on, and Farley's other hand moved to his lap and began rooting in his boxer shorts.

"I just want to sit here a minute, baby, with you," he whispered. "I won't say a word, and . . ." The hand in his lap began to move. He pivoted slightly on the bed, the better to

166

follow the progress of his other hand, now making its way up Jack's shin, to her knee, where it rested like a weary traveler. "And you won't say a word. Not a word, just lie there like my own sweet girl, my best little"—the hand in his lap moved faster now, up from his shorts and down again quick—"girl." His breathing grew louder, harsher, and Tex heard him grunt as the hand on Jack's leg moved on, following the soft guide of her thigh, testing it the way his mother squeezed fruit, creeping onward to the hem of her nightshirt.

Jack didn't move. She didn't speak. She looked dead again, and now Tex wished it were true, or that he was dead, or at least that this nightmare would end and he'd wake up in his room with sunshine blasting through the windows and the smell of the day's ball game already in his nostrils instead of this other smell, this mixture of Jack's dirty socks, Willa May's crib, and Farley, his cigar- and beer-scented stink, and something stronger, a ripeness that made Tex think of creatures burrowing in river mud, cracking open crawdads with tiny hands and sharp white teeth. A bitter substance rose in his throat, but he didn't look away. Farley's hand was higher now, and Jack's nightshirt with it, while his other hand seemed to pound the breath out of him, and Tex couldn't look away even as the nightshirt rode higher, exposing a region of milky thigh he'd never seen before, and a little higher yet, until he was staring helplessly at her underpants, patternless and clean and white as her skin.

A moan filled the room and Farley hunched forward suddenly, as if suffering a blow to the back of the head. He collapsed over himself and Jack's legs, the one hand clutching her thigh while the other pounded on, until a great sob bubbled from his throat and he grabbed quickly for her bedsheet, pulled it to his lap, and shuddered horribly once, and once again.

He took a moment catching his breath. Then, his back still to her face, he composed himself, ran a hand through his hair, and stood up. The mattress gave the identical sad creak of springs, and Tex saw that Jack looked exactly the same, except for the nightshirt, which remained as her father had left it, hiked up to her hip. A wake of foul air forced itself into the closet as Farley passed by, and then he was gone, closing the door behind him more quietly, even, than a dropped cotton ball.

When he finally stood up, Tex discovered that his legs were like wood, utterly numb from crouching, as if they weren't even his. His arms felt the same way. Even his head. He felt as if he'd been thoroughly taken apart, then reassembled by idiots, his left hand on his right arm, eyes reversed, his brain plopped back into his skull upside down. He wanted to cry and vomit at the same time.

At last he stepped out of the closet, feeling more exposed, for some reason, than Jack looked in her hitched-up nightshirt. She lay there blinking at the ceiling, and he knew that as soon as he was gone she'd find her glove and that Spalding, lie back in her polluted sheets, and begin her game of catch.

The bile was in his throat again—only it wasn't bile, or at least it didn't come out that way. It came out in English.

"Why didn't you stop him?"

She rolled her face toward him, her eyes dull and hateful, rolled it slowly back. She pinched the hem of her nightshirt, lifted it, and returned it to its full length.

"Why," she asked the ceiling, "didn't you?"

18

The bike moved and his legs moved along with it, sense-lessly mechanical, through the blue night. How did he get here? He thought hard to remember, but it was as if his brain were divided by a thin wall that would not allow the one half, the half that wanted to know, to look into the other half, the half that knew. He knew and he didn't—and didn't want to—and didn't know why—and did. He'd seen something impossible, something that couldn't be true, yet there it was, prowling the back of his skull like a sick dog, letting him forget for a few minutes, only to rush out from the shadows and sink its teeth.

Why *didn't* he stop him?

Well, that was easy enough: he was Farley. His stepfather. His coach. A man who'd punched Ray Stucky to the ground.

And maybe that would've been better. Maybe he'd have beaten the entire scene from Tex's memory. Maybe he'd have killed him.

He rode on, but the moon kept with him, a bright un-blinking eyeball over his right shoulder. The farther he got from town, the brighter it seemed to shine, until it hurt his eyes even to look at it. He pedaled out to the middle of the Route 61 bridge, halfway to Illinois, to rest his eyes in the dark flow of the Mississippi. But the inky water sent such a spike of dread through his heart he flew back to shore as if the bridge were collapsing, section by section, just behind his rear tire.

Back in Iowa, he rode along the highway, watching the slow approach of headlights. He was glad for the company even when drivers honked and called him a retard, but then when they passed, leaving him alone with the moon, it was like plunging back into a deep pit. He wished Jack were riding alongside him, the way they'd ridden together all summer, but then he remembered why he was out here and knew they'd never ride together like that again. How could they? How could he ever face her? He thought of his own father and wanted to drop everything he knew in his hands and say, *Here: I kept my eyes open. Now fix it.*

Then a new thought occurred to him, almost as terrible as the sight of Farley's hand on Jack's leg. How could he tell what he'd seen without confessing how he'd seen it?

Up ahead a pale haze began to gather strength as he pedaled, distinguishing itself from moonlight. He rode toward this haze, and before he fully understood where his bike had taken him, he'd left moonlight behind and coasted into the super-illuminated, bug-swarmed parking lot of the Route 61 Diner.

Every moth and flying beetle in Iowa was there, fighting for the chance to bounce its head off a pair of lofty, humming lamps. Into this buggy snowstorm nighthawks and whippoorwills repeatedly dove, struck, and dove again. For bugs and birds the Route 61 Diner was the place to be, but only one car, Tex observed, had come to rest in its light: an old green Chevy Impala. And the owner of that car, he knew, wasn't here to eat. She was here to serve.

He propped his bike against the trunk of a lamppost and snuck up on plate glass. He didn't know why, but he wanted to see her again. And if Ray Stucky was in there keeping her company, he wanted to see that, too. He wanted to see what he never got to see that day in the courthouse: Stucky's everyday, unrehearsed face. The one Farley smashed with his fist.

But the diner was empty, nothing moving but three metal ceiling fans and steam from a globe of coffee back behind the cash register.

They're in the kitchen, Tex speculated, *reenacting that night at her apartment.* Then, as he stood there looking through his own reflection, an aluminum door swept open and a woman in a white uniform stepped into view. A rusty ponytail swung, two coffee-bean eyes homed in on him more quickly than bugs to light, and Lucinda Barnes stopped in her tracks. Tex stared back, paralyzed, until she put her hands on her hips and cocked her head. *Well,* her posture asked, *comin' in, or what?*

He stepped away from the glass, and went in.

"Sit anywhere you want," she called, digging in silverware.

He decided against orange, mushroom-shaped barstools and settled into a brown Naugahyde booth by the front window where he could keep an eye on his bike. Overhead, a ceiling fan stirred up the odors of bacon grease, cigarettes, old coffee. A circular fluorescent bulb flickered like a sick halo.

"You need a menu?" she asked, suddenly beside him. "Or are you here for the world-famous coffee?" If she recognized him as the son of Ray Stucky's lawyer, she didn't show it.

Tex stared at pink Formica and said coffee would be fine.

"That was a joke, hon."

"Black, please."

"Suit yourself." She whirled, adding cinnamon gum to the mixture of smells, and went to pour the first cup of coffee of his life. She returned with two cups, used one to indicate the unoccupied side of his booth. "Do you mind?" He shook his head and she sat down as if she'd been waiting all night—for many nights—for permission to do so.

Tex lifted his cup to his lips and sipped the hot, bitter liquid. "Delicious," he said.

She took a sip and looked him over. "You get lost coming home from the ballpark?" He followed her gaze back to himself and realized he was wearing his Twins uniform. He didn't remember putting it on.

"Forgot to change," he said.

"That happens." She waited for him to look up, then smiled. Her brown eyes were softer than coffee beans, more like caramels. "Sometimes," she confided, "I'm so tired when I get home, I wake up wearing this."

He nodded and looked away, toward the door. Mentally he was already on his bike and burning rubber. He'd take the glare of the moon over her white uniform any day.

She observed him a moment, and sighed. "Listen, I've had a long night. If you're running away from home, why don't you just say so. Lots of kids get this far before going back. I can either call your folks to come get you, or you can wait around till six, when Denise comes in, and I'll drop you off myself." She nodded toward his bike in the parking lot. "I got a trunk big as a closet."

He choked down a swig of coffee. "I'm not running away," he said. "I'm just out riding."

"Oh." She wiped something from the table. "Sorry." They both stared into coffee. "You got a name?" she asked.

"Yes."

"May I ask what it is, since I don't see your name tag."

He hesitated. "Tex."

"As in Texas?"

"It's a nickname."

"Tex what?"

"Donleavy," he said without hesitating. "As in Jacob P."

She took a moment taking this in. He was prepared for her to screw up her face in disgust, to cuss him and kick him out. But she just sat there, calmly eyeing him.

"You know who I am?" she asked.

"I know about your . . . case, if that's what you mean. I saw you at the trial. On the stand."

"What'd you go and do a thing like that for?"

He tried to meet her eyes but couldn't for more than a heartbeat. "It's a public place."

"So's the crapper at the bus depot."

"The what?"

"Never mind." She closed her eyes and kept them closed a long time, her tinted eyelids a sore reminder of Jack pretending to be asleep. Tex swished coffee around in his cup and had no idea what he should say or if he was even supposed to try, or if he was supposed to just sit there quietly enduring her presence, his punishment for being his father's son. At last she opened her eyes again, and he had the feeling, looking into them, that she'd had a good cry, dried her eyes, and felt a whole world better, thank you, all behind the curtains of her eyelids.

"Look," she said, "I don't hold nothin' against your daddy, I really don't. He was just doing his job. Fact is, the only person I got to blame for the whole mess is me."

Tex considered this, but had to reject it. "Just 'cause he got acquitted doesn't mean he didn't do what you said."

"I know, sweetie. And thank you. Before the trial there weren't but two people who could ever really know what happened. Now, thanks to *due process*, everybody *thinks* they know. I mean, you should've seen the business we were getting in here for a while! Better than the carnival."

Tex was confused, a thickness filling his head in a way that made him want to lay it down. "But you had to do it," he said. "You had to. He broke the law."

"Now you sound like my lawyer." She sat up straight, made herself male and pompous. " 'The Ray Stuckys of the world are counting on your lack of fortitude, Ms. Barnes!' " She relaxed again. "He said I had a moral whatchamacallit. Imperative. Said that with his help we could change the course of legal history in Iowa." She smiled with real amusement.

"He even had this idea that, someday, a man could go to jail for, you know"—she lowered her voice—"taking liberties with his own wife."

What about his daughter? Tex wondered, and he couldn't help it, he had to cover his face with his hands. It felt good under there, dark, and he realized how easily he could fall asleep, how much he wanted to, the only end he could think of to thoughts that kept diving like birds into his brain.

He felt her watching him, trying to figure out, possibly, where a kid his age got such an overdeveloped sense of right and wrong that he had to bury his face in his hands. When he put them back on the table, she covered them in hers. "I hate to say it, Tex, but the fact is the whole world's got their dirty little secrets. Most folks just don't go dragging them into a courtroom."

He endured the sensation as long as he could, then pulled both hands free and sat on them, his head lowered as if brooding seriously on what she'd told him and not on the thought he couldn't keep down any longer, the thought the touch of her fingers had dug loose, finally, from the silt of his skull. He knew why he hadn't stopped him, and it had nothing to do with fear. He hadn't stopped him because, horrified as he'd been by the sight of Farley's hand on Jack's leg, he'd also been fascinated and envious. He'd wanted to touch her himself.

Farley had told him once that they were all ballplayers of one kind or another. But as Tex sat in a booth with Lucinda Barnes, he knew they were not all ballplayers of one kind or another. They were all Ray Stuckys.

19

He'd gone down in slow motion, as if sinking to the bottom of a grassy pond, but the moment his head came to rest on the seat, time jumped ahead and he was tugged back to consciousness on a line of steamy daylight, hooked by the sound and smell of bacon spattering on a grill. For a moment he continued to lie there, facedown, listening to the drone of strange voices, the music of forks and knives, wondering where they'd all come from.

At last he turned his head toward the other side of the booth, and the first thing he thought was that Lucinda Barnes was still over there, and the second was that she had the skinniest legs he'd ever seen on a grown woman. Then he saw a small brown scab stuck to one knee like an old penny, and he knew who the legs belonged to. He sat up, banging his head on the table along the way.

"That had to hurt."

He scowled at the top of her Cardinals cap, but she

couldn't be bothered to look up, engrossed as she was by the sports page. He heard the squeak of rubber soles on linoleum and turned to see Lucinda Barnes's replacement, Denise, a large, brown-skinned woman nimbly serving steaming eggs and pancakes and coffee. Neither she nor her customers seemed to care much about Tex and Jack; nobody knew the things they knew, not even the sun, now flooding the diner with a crazy yellow light.

"What're you doing here?" he said.

She looked up at last and he was startled by the paleness of her face, as if summer had come off with a good scrubbing. Puffy, bluish half-moons hung below her eyes.

"Looking for you," she said. "And don't congratulate me."

He remembered his bike and looked outside. It was where he'd left it, a dead giveaway. Jack had leaned her Huffy against it, her handlebars entwined in his in a weird, unsightly way.

Denise squeaked over and shook her head. "Finally up, huh? Your sister been waiting here the better part of two hours. I expect you're both well past starved." She laid out a pair of menus.

"Go ahead and order," Jack said. "I brought money."

"No thanks. *Sis.* Not hungry."

"You sure?" Denise asked. "Lucy said all you drunk all morning was coffee." She jabbed a pen in the direction of his uniform. "Now, how you gonna play ball on nothing but Sanka?"

One of her subjects, food or baseball or coffee, caused a dangerous ballooning in his stomach, and it was all Tex could do to fight it down and order ice water. Jack ordered blueberry pancakes with extra butter, and Denise squeaked away.

"How long you been looking?" he asked when they were alone.

"Since about ten minutes after you ditched out."

"Ditched out?" He coughed up a laugh. "Ditched outta what?"

"Don't be a jerk, Tex."

"*I'm* a jerk? How am I a jerk, after that—" He jabbed his thumb in the general direction of his mother's house. "I mean I feel like I'm gonna barf, right here."

Her shrug was a weak one. "Don't let me stop you."

He ran The Hand through his greasy hair. "Why didn't you, why don't you just . . ."

She stared at him, and he got the idea she'd happily sink a butter knife into his throat. "Why don't I just what?"

"*Tell* somebody."

"Like who?"

"Like my mom, for starters."

She looked away. "Tried that once."

"You told my mom?"

"Not yours. Mine."

"*Your* mom? Wait . . ." He shook his head, unwilling to believe it. "It's been going on that long?"

"*I* don't know how long it's been going on, Tex. All I know is when I first started feeling crummy about it. I felt crummy about it a long time before I did anything."

He waited. "What'd you do?"

She took a breath. "I didn't plan it or anything. But one

day I just walked out of school, got on the bus, and went to the hospital. And the next thing I know I'm bawling my eyes out, telling her how Daddy's doing this stuff, how he's coming into my room at night, and all that crap."

Tex watched her, riveted. "What'd she say?"

"Nothin'. She didn't say a thing. She weighed about ten pounds by then and had all these tubes running into her, but she reached up and just, kind of, slapped me. Across the face."

Tex flinched. His own face burned, as if Jack had demonstrated.

Denise delivered glasses of ice water, and moved on.

"My mom wouldn't do that," Tex said. "She'd help you."

"Maybe she'd go right out and divorce him, then he'd hate me for that, too."

"Hate you? Seems to me he likes you too much."

She wrapped her fingers around her glass but didn't lift it, as if she didn't have the strength. "In the light of day he hates me," she said. "You should know, you only been watching it all summer."

Tex picked up his water and gulped, trying to understand. "You think he hates you because you're a girl? Because you can't play real ball? Because of some stupid rules? Well, listen, there's something you don't know—"

"It's more than baseball, Tex. It's more than a damn *game*. A guy like Farley doesn't know how to talk to a girl, and ever since my mom died, he's stopped even trying. For a while he even stopped coming into my room. But then he'll go and get drunk, get himself all wound up, and Caroline—I'm not blaming her—but she'll fall dead asleep with wine, and in he comes again, making me realize I didn't make it all up, or dream it." He watched her knuckles, so white with gripping her glass he was sure she'd break it. "That's why he hates me, Tex. 'Cause I'm not what he ever wanted and 'cause I make him think of something else. I give him bad ideas. I can't help it, but I do. Seems like I'm always giving people bad ideas."

"It's not your fault he comes into your room, Jack. He's just a fat, sick—" He looked down, saw his own greasy fingerprints on Formica. "Ain't your fault what I did, either."

"What you did?"

"At the river. Talk about bad ideas."

She fished a cube of ice from her glass, popped it into her mouth. "Tex," she said around the cube, "don't you go feeling bad about that. What happened was okay by me."

"That doesn't make it right."

Denise returned with pancakes, and after she was gone they both sat there watching a giant slug of butter make its way to the edge of the plate.

"This is what my dad told me to look out for," he said.

Jack looked up, puzzled, and he went on to explain his instructions from that day she fell asleep on his father's sofa: how Tex was supposed to keep his eyes open for something he'd only know when, and if, he saw it. It seemed so obvious now he couldn't believe he hadn't figured it out sooner. All those nights in his bed, hearing things. It didn't take a genius.

He said, "You must've told my dad something about Farley."

She doused her pancakes in syrup. "I didn't tell him anything about this." She thunked down the syrup and glared at him. "And neither will you. Him or anybody else. Promise, Tex."

"How else is it gonna stop?"

"I don't know, but I do know it ain't nobody's business but mine. I mean it, Tex. Now promise."

"He should be arrested. Thrown in jail."

"Oh, great idea. That way the whole town can know. Thanks, Tex. I knew I could count on you."

He tried to concentrate, but the right thing to do bobbed away from him like an apple in water, and he was blindfolded and had no teeth anyway. All he knew for sure was that he had no intention of telling anyone ever that he'd been hiding in Jack's closet, and who'd believe him otherwise? He'd be just another Lucinda Barnes, and the whole town would see him—all of them, Jack and Farley and his mother and Tex—the way they saw her.

He hung his head and promised, at last, not to tell.

Jack nodded and dug into her breakfast. He watched her eat, sick to his stomach.

"Why didn't you run away that day you had the chance?"

She returned a dripping triangle of pancake to her plate. "I don't know."

"Yes you do." He waited. He'd wait there all day, he meant to let her know. But in a moment she looked up, and didn't look away.

"Think I could just leave her like that, all alone in that house?"

"That's why we gotta tell her!" he blurted. "So she can get the hell out of there, get as far away from that pig as—"

Jack's expression cut him off. She was staring at him like he was the most hopeless, clueless thing she'd ever seen.

"You're not talking about my mom," he said.

She shook her head and turned to the window, and Tex looked, too, as if he might actually see the little girl all the way from here.

Somewhere in his mother's photo albums was a snapshot of the three of them, Tex and his parents, standing before a small cinder-block building with a large plate-glass window still bearing beef prices and the legend MASON'S MEATS. In the picture, Tex stood between his mother and father, a waif with one hand buried in his pocket, while in the glass behind them hovered the spectral image of Mrs. Mason, retained by his mother to capture the moment on film. These days the plate-glass window read, in small gold lettering, JACOB P. DONLEAVY, ATTORNEY-AT-LAW, but the spirit of meat lived on, and when Tex arrived, Jacob was at his desk eating a cheeseburger.

At last he looked up and motioned the boy in, told him to have a seat. "I think you'll find my rates very reasonable." Tex sat but couldn't look his father in the eye, turned instead to read the titles of uniform volumes that covered all of one wall like bricks and mortar. "And of course if I can't help you with your problem," his father continued, "there'll be no charge for this initial consultation."

"I'm not here for advice," Tex said.

"No? A social call? I'd think you'd be home washing that uniform, getting ready for the game."

"I could care less about the game."

"And why's that?"

"Because I could, that's why."

Jacob nodded. He offered the cheeseburger. "Hungry?" Tex wasn't, and Jacob wrapped up the remainder and dropped it with a bang into a metal wastebasket. "Well, you've had an impressive season nonetheless. I'm very proud." He shuffled papers. "And soon, I take it, you'll be coming home."

"I'm already home," Tex said, slumping some in the chair. "I mean, if it's all right with you."

"Of course it is. As a matter of fact, to be honest—"

"What about Linda?"

"What about her?"

"I don't wanna be in the way."

Jacob peered at him over his glasses. "Tex. You could never be an inconvenience to me or to her, even if she were around to be inconvenienced, which, as it happens, she is not."

They stared at each other for several seconds, but Tex still didn't get it.

"I'm afraid we won't be seeing Miss Volesky anymore, Tex."

A red Mustang charged into Tex's brain, tore through a guardrail, and plunged into black water. "What do you mean?"

"I mean . . ." Jacob glanced at his watch. "I mean she has reconciled with her husband."

"Husband?" The word was worse, somehow, than a car crash. "You mean she was *married*?"

Jacob laced his fingers atop a text that lay open before him. "According to the law, yes." He continued to stare at his son, not very pleased, clearly, by what he was seeing. "They'd been separated for some time, Tex."

"And you knew about it—about him—the whole time?"

"Of course. I was her attorney."

Lucinda Barnes was suddenly in Tex's ear, reminding him that everybody, even his own father, had their dirty little secrets. He stared at the cracks in the ceiling and felt on the brink of throwing some kind of fit. "And so—that's it? She's just gone?"

"Well . . . yes."

"Did you even talk to her? Did she even say anything?"

"Of course, Tex. We talked quite a lot. Though, finally, there's nothing much one can say. She had to do what she had to do."

Tex waited for his father to go on. He waited for him to show some indication that he felt the way Tex felt, like he'd just been hit in the chest by a fastball.

"Well," Tex said at last, disgusted with everybody. "That's just great. That's just perfect."

Jacob sat back in his chair and removed his glasses. He rubbed the bridge of his nose for some time, replaced the glasses, and leaned forward again.

"Son," he said, "what did you come to tell me?"

Tex met his gaze and forgot about Linda. He was back in that closet, wide-eyed and shaking and unable to breathe.

"Something I can't," he said, looking away.

"Because you made a promise."

He nodded before he could stop himself. His father waited for him to go on, but Tex had become part of the chair. His father could get nothing more out of him if he didn't move or talk or even blink. A small crystal and brass desk clock, a long-ago birthday present from Tex and his mother, ticked away like a time bomb.

Jacob gave up and turned to the book on his desk. Flipped a page, flipped it back. He raised a knuckle to his lips as if preparing to seize a bishop. "I was just reading, before you stopped by, about this thing called mandated reporting. Very interesting." He glanced up, then went on as if Tex had begged him to. "Mandated reporting, Tex, means that when professional people, such as teachers or doctors or police officers, suspect that a child's welfare is endangered in some way, because they see injuries, or the child tells them, or for any other reason—if they suspect a child is in danger, then they're required by law to report it to the authorities."

Tex watched his father watching him, wondering if he could see the sparks of panic he felt jumping off his skull.

"That's the legal, statutory mandate," Jacob added, as if to put his fears to rest, "which doesn't apply to regular folks like you and me. The law doesn't oblige folks like us to make reports of child endangerment, Tex. But it allows it."

It was no use, Tex knew. He'd go on and on until Tex said something. "You want me to break my promise," he said.

Jacob tapped fingers against his lips, deliberating. "I want you to think about the Hobson's choice you're facing here." Tex remembered the term from the beginning of the summer, when his father had told him about Jackie Robinson—but his father wasn't counting on it. "You feel ethically bound to keep your promise," he said, "and I wouldn't want you to feel any other way. But there's another ethical issue at stake, and the conflict you face is which one presents the greater obligation: should you keep your promise to that girl or break it for her own safety and welfare?"

Tex's heart sank. Jack had just officially entered the room. "And you think it'd be for her own safety and welfare," he asked, unable to control the tremble in his voice, "to go dragging everybody into a courtroom? Have the whole town knowing all about it?"

Jacob gave him a second to collect himself. "The likelihood of any kind of trial is almost nil, Tex. Even if a hearing were required, it would be completely closed to the public." Tex looked away, toward the door, but the force of his father's eyes pulled him back. "I promise you, Tex. There are ways Jack and her father can both be helped without anyone ever hearing a word about it."

Now Farley was in the room and Tex could hardly breathe. "You talk like you know," he said. "Like you know everything. Why do you need me?"

"Because I need to have what this book calls a 'reasonable belief' that that girl is in danger, and all I have so far is a reasonable suspicion. You, on the other hand, know for certain."

"I never said that."

"Tex," he said with a smile. "We've known each other an awful long time. I bet I know the scars on your right hand almost as well as you do. And I'm pretty sure it wasn't boredom made you come here today. You came to tell me what I asked you to keep an eye out for, and I'm proud you did. I wish to God you never had to, but now that you have, well . . ." He shook his head, the way he always did before he said the word *checkmate*, as though it caused him great pain to say it, but what could he do? "Now I need to know the answer to your dilemma," he said. "I need to know before I can take the next step."

Tex thought about dropping his head to his desk and bawling. Papers and books and clocks would be swept to the floor with the flood of his tears.

Instead he took a breath and swallowed hard. "Can I have some time to think about it?"

His father hesitated, then nodded. "On one condition."

"What."

Jacob adjusted his glasses and returned his finger to a line of text, as if he'd merely paused in his reading. "You get that uniform into a washing machine. You've got a big game to-day."

20

It was the last thing Tex expected to see.

At the same time, it didn't surprise him at all. On a day like this one, when everything was so strange and terrible you weren't even sure you were awake, a red Mustang in your driveway almost made sense. She'd changed her mind, was all. She'd made a mistake, and now she was waiting for his father to come home to tell him, and later they'd cook a big dinner and she'd stay over and everything would be normal again.

He dumped his bike and went in to keep her company.

But she wasn't downstairs—and he did not want to go looking for her upstairs—so he went to the kitchen to grab something to drink and wait it out. He had his head in the fridge when she walked in and screamed.

Tex screamed, too. "What!"

"Tex!"

"What!"

She flattened her hand against her chest. "You scared the crap outta me!"

"Sorry."

"What are you doing here?" She gave a tug to her purse strap, and Tex noticed the bundle of clothes in her other arm, blue jeans and T-shirts, and the tennis shoes on her feet.

He let go of the refrigerator door, watched it suck itself shut. "I was just in town," he said. "Talking to Dad."

"Oh." She took her lower lip between her teeth, bit down hard. "Did he . . . did you talk about . . ."

"Yeah." Tex swiped at some filth on his uniform. "He told me."

"Oh," she said again. Her cheeks grew round, then deflated in a noisy gust. She began shaking her head as if she'd just heard some long, implausible story. "Pretty weird, huh?" He shrugged, and she raised her eyebrows. "You don't think so?"

"I've seen weirder," he almost said, but thought better of it. Talking with his father had given him the idea that anybody could tell exactly what was on his mind just by looking at him, and he didn't want to make it any easier by opening his mouth.

"Well," Linda said. "I'm sorry, anyway, Tex. I wish I could explain it, but I can't. It's just what happens to people." He must have looked at her funny, he thought, like he didn't believe her, for she went on, in an expert tone, "You too, someday. Trust me. You'll meet some girl and you won't know up from down. You'll do stuff you never, *ever* thought you'd do, and you'll get hurt, but you'll live, *somehow*, and you'll find someone else, but you'll never be really, truly happy no matter what, and that's how you'll know you're human."

If she was trying to tell his fortune, Tex thought, he

wished she wouldn't bother. All he wanted to know about was the next few hours, the next day, the day after that. All he wanted to know about was Jack.

"But that's very gloomy, isn't it?" Linda said with a shooing gesture. Then she reached out and took The Hand in hers, and he guessed she meant to take a closer look, to see what she could see in those scars. But she didn't look, she just held The Hand, her fingertips somehow both cool and hot on his skin, and smiled at him. "I'm just so glad I got to see you, Tex. I'm so glad I got to say goodbye. You're an amazing kid, and I'm going to miss you like crazy!"

He didn't know what to say to that. Or what to do when she raised The Hand to her face and kissed his knuckles. He didn't know what to do after the door banged shut and the Mustang rumbled to life, or what to do when the sound of its engine grew so faint he couldn't tell it from the hum of the refrigerator.

Finally, robotically, he moved across the kitchen, opened a door, and went down to the basement. And only then did he think: *accident.*

Meeting her today was a pure accident. If he hadn't just happened by, he never would've seen her at all. She would've just disappeared.

That's the kind of world it was today, he observed, pulling off his uniform. Today, entire people, and everything you ever knew about them, or ever felt, could just drop out of your life forever, like stones to the bottom of a river.

"Hey, stranger." His mother smiled up at him from the kitchen table. "We were getting worried." They were all there,

191

unchanged, eating an early dinner of beans and hot dogs. Farley glanced up to take note of his uniform—clean, now, if not entirely dry—and said, "Cutting it close, son."

"Don't call me that," Tex wanted to say. He stared at him, hoping Farley would glance up again, this time into his eyes, where he'd surely see Tex's knowledge, and his hatred. But he didn't glance up, and neither did Jack. She just sat there, looking to Tex like someone who'd decided never to come to another dinner table again without something to read. Only his mother paid him any attention, smiling at him as if he'd been gone for years and she was very pleased with how he'd turned out. The more she beamed at him, the more he wanted to say, "Stop it! Stop smiling like everything's fine, like this isn't the craziest house on the planet!" But he'd no sooner thought this than he felt kicked in the head by the obvious: she didn't know. She still trusted, maybe even loved Farley Dickerson.

He held her gaze until her smile faded and she began to blink. "You must be starved," she said, setting down her fork. She dabbed at the corners of her mouth and pushed up from the table.

How could she not know? he wondered. How could anyone be so stupid?

"No time for pampering," Farley said. "Those Pirates aren't gonna just hand that pennant over."

"He has to eat," Caroline said.

"Sure he does. But he knows the score: he missed dinner and it's game time. He made his choice." Farley eyed him critically but there was warmth in the look, as if it caused him great pleasure to admonish Tex this way: coach to ballplayer.

Man to man. Father to son. A splinter of the way Tex used to feel for him pricked at his heart, and he wished he'd never had to come back here, ever. But he'd had to, this one last time, for his cap and his cleats and his mitt. And to make sure he got to the park on time.

"I ain't hungry," he said.

"You're *not* hungry," Caroline said.

"No," he said, stepping around her to the refrigerator. "I *ain't*." He grabbed a Coke and forced The Hand to pry it open.

"See there?" Farley said. "The boy's got his priorities straight as a nail. And look at Jack, here." They all did. "Just sitting there reading away while the clock ticks on, knowing full well she should be changing her clothes."

"Something wrong with the way I'm dressed?"

Tex knew where this was going. He'd tried to tell her about it back at the Route 61 Diner, when she said Farley didn't love her.

"Only one small thing," Farley said.

She looked up, defiant. "Which is?"

He snuck Tex a wink. "It ain't regulation, darlin'."

Jacob waited in the bleachers, looking somehow more alien and isolated than ever in his wing tips and tie. Seeing him, Tex was suddenly struck by an advance sense of loneliness, of what it would be like when this game was over and it was just the two of them again in that big house. What would they ever do without Linda's smile, her lilac scent, and her laughter filling the rooms?

Jacob rose at their approach and offered the usual pleasantries, including a handshake with Farley. To all appearances it was just another day at the ballpark, and Tex allowed himself the dismal hope that, for some reason, his father no longer wished to know what he knew.

Jacob gave Jack the once-over and smiled with real pleasure. "You look very different in a blue cap, Jack."

"Feel different." She made an adjustment to her jersey, and Tex saw that she was still annoyed, embarrassed, and nervous.

"Whose crazy idea was this?" she'd demanded back at the house.

"We took a vote and decided you should play," Tex had said. "Seeing as how it might be our last game and all."

"Who took a vote?"

"We did. The Twins."

She narrowed her eyes. "You saying the whole team wants me to play in the game?"

"An overwhelming majority," Farley said. "Like it or not, there's still one or two backward-thinking elements in our ranks."

"But the rules—" she began, but Farley would hear no more bellyaching. "You let me worry about the rules," he'd said with finality.

If it were possible, he'd found an even larger uniform for her than he'd found for Tex, and no one without X-ray vision would be able to detect, beneath the billows of fabric, the body of a thirteen-year-old girl. The rules could be broken, Tex understood, without anyone ever knowing.

Now Farley sent Jack off to the outfield, where most of the

Twins were already paired, and she fell into place like an egg in a carton.

When Farley got done with it, the lineup card looked like the work of a madman, and Jack's name was buried deep in the mess. He assigned her to right field, the game's loneliest and therefore safest position, then made a point of reminding his players that she would not be offended, would in fact be much obliged, if they used the traditional "Attaboy!" where she was concerned. Finally, he claimed to be proud, damn proud, no matter the outcome, of each and every one of them. In ten years of coaching he'd never known a finer group of ballplayers. The Twins piled up their hands, gave the cheer, then took the field as if they couldn't wait to win the pennant for him, as if they'd never dreamed of anything less.

"How's she feeling today, son?" Farley asked, joining Tex on the mound. He dug up a pebble with the point of his cowboy boot, banished it from the mound. "You got the stuff?"

Tex rolled his shoulder and turned to Wrigley. "Let's go one heat, two slider, and three curve. Okay?"

"Okay."

Farley clapped both boys on the back. He glanced around the park and took a deep breath through his nostrils. "Helluva perfect day for a ball game." He pulled a long plastic cylinder from his shirt pocket and showed it to the boys. "See this cigar? It's Cuban, and I can't even tell you how much it cost because you wouldn't believe it." He put the cylinder back in his pocket and gave it a pat, smiling vaguely.

Wrigley looked at Tex, dumbfounded and pale. Tex surprised himself by winking, and some color returned to the kid's doughy face. Tex turned to Farley. "Have your matches ready."

Farley grinned, smacked their backs again, and finally left the mound. Tex watched him go.

"You ready?" Wrigley said from far off. "Tex?"

Tex dragged his eyes from Farley and brought Wrigley into focus. He looked into the kid's nervous blue eyes and felt his resolve stumble, a strange trembling in the knees. But another glance toward the bench, where Farley now stood with his arms crossed, beaming confidence and gusto, snapped him out of it.

"Just remember one thing," Tex told his catcher. "Nobody on God's green ballpark can beat us, except us."

The first Pirate batter came to the plate and flashed Tex a familiar, metallic grin. It was Silver Tooth, the kid from the carnival. Tex stole a glance into right field and was satisfied: not even Jack would recognize herself out there.

Silver Tooth kept on grinning, and that glint caused such a blur of hatred that Tex didn't even try to read his catcher's signs. He just threw the ball three times as hard as he could and the kid swung three times and that was that. No more silver.

Fans cheered, but Farley and the Twins kept their cool; they had seventeen outs to go. The next batter turned Tex's curveball into a double down the third-base foul line, and a few Twins found their voices. "No sweat, Tex. Lucky swing."

Tex walked off the mound and back, cursing the laces of his cleats.

"Shake it off, Tex," Farley called. "Just pitch 'em in there, son."

Tex took his advice, heaving a melon of such size and ripeness it was a wonder the ball did not explode into mush. Instead it described a low rainbow over the infield, dropped between Jack and Gomez and sped on until it was stopped, audibly, by the picket fence. The runner scored, and only a brilliant throw from Gomez, finally, kept the batter from rounding third.

Wrigley trundled up to the mound, mask in hand. "You're rushing your windup."

"Windup my ass." Dunsmore had joined them. "Coach oughtta yank him before we get blown outta here."

"Who asked you?" Wrigley said. "He's just working out the kinks. Right, Tex?"

"Right," Tex said. "Just working out the kinks."

"Work 'em out faster, will ya? I wanna bat before dark."

Wrigley watched Dunsmore go, then spit inexpertly at the dirt. "Don't let him get to you."

Tex fought back the smile. "Don't worry."

The next batter popped up to center, but the one after that creamed Tex's slider, igniting a first-inning rally that showed no signs of ending until Silver Tooth was back at the plate. Not grinning, this time.

Tex worked up a full count, and was actually considering giving the creep his base—when he did it again. Out came the silver, and Tex threw with so much force he felt a pop in his shoulder. Silver Tooth walked away cursing and Tex retreated to the bench, confident the game was in his hands.

But he had not counted on his teammates. Burger stepped up and doubled to left, and Frog brought him home with a line drive just over the mitt of his counterpart at short. Gomez popped up to center field, Frog advanced to third on the tag-up, and Dunsmore headed for the plate.

He paused on the other side of the fence. "This guy looks about as hard to hit as you, Davy."

Tex shrugged.

He tried again. "Know what I'm gonna do with the first piece of fruit he throws me?"

"Hit it?"

Dunsmore stared at him, his grin fading. He looked as if he was thinking about dropping everything and beating the crap out of Tex, just for the hell of it. But the ump barked, "Batter up!" and Dunsmore continued on to the plate. He took a big swing at the shadow of a curveball, beat his bat once in the dirt, and fouled off another.

"Easy does it, Big D," Farley advised from third base. "Wait for a straight one."

Dunsmore dug in and the pitcher finished him off with a nice, late-dropping slider.

Spinelli made contact, but the Pirate second baseman dug up the grounder and ended the inning with a lazy throw to first.

Tex jumped to his feet and returned to the mound. A moment later, with a hard thump to his chest, he saw Farley crossing the infield. He came up on the mound, stood so close Tex could smell his sweat. Wrigley made a move to join them, but Farley waved him away.

"Feeling okay, Tex?"

"I feel fine."

"Seemed a little tight that first inning."

"It was just—you know. Nerves." He took a breath. "I'm okay now."

Farley studied him, nodded, and returned, finally, to the bench.

His team still down by four, Tex pitched as well as he could in the second inning, but every time he threw he felt the pop in his shoulder, and the Pirates seemed to hear it. They got their bats around on his fastball, straightened out his curves, watched his sliders dive into dirt. Before the inning was over he'd given up two more runs.

At the bench, sweating furiously, Farley attempted to inspire. "Those are just boys out there, you guys! A bunch of damn boys no older or bigger or faster or stronger or smarter than you. Hell, you've whipped teams twice as good as they are now when you were half as good yourselves, you know you have. Now let's get our heads together and start playing like the Minnesota Twins, how about it?"

Zimmerman was sufficiently terrorized to actually swing his bat. Somehow, he connected, and Jacob welcomed him to first base with an uncharacteristic swat to the pants.

Tex followed, but swinging the bat only aggravated his shoulder, and he stood by as the third strike crossed the plate.

Jack met him on his way back to the bench, took his helmet, and replaced him at the plate, all as if she'd done it a million times.

The pitcher checked Zimmerman at first, then stretched

and heaved his fastball. Jack took her cut and the ball fouled off skyward, up and over the backstop. She watched it go, smiling, marveling.

"Good swing, batter," Farley noted. "Let him pitch to you, now."

Jack adjusted her helmet and dug in. She showed the pitcher where she wanted the ball, and he nodded.

But then, before he could begin his stretch, someone yelled from the outfield, and everyone turned to see the Pirate left fielder jogging in.

"Time!" the kid called again. Silver glinted in the sun. "Time out, Ump!"

21

The ump raised a palm to the pitcher, and Jack stepped
from the box. Farley and his players watched as Silver Tooth
said something into his coach's ear, then shadowed him out
onto the infield.

"What's the big idea, Dickerson?" The coach was slightly
built, not much bigger than his player, and he tried to put on
a few inches and pounds with the force of his voice, but it
didn't take: no amount of volume could obscure the look of a
man who'd grown up being pushed down by bigger boys.

Somehow, rising from the bench, Farley looked even less
menacing. He sank his hands in his pockets and hunched his
shoulders, as if he were poorly dressed on a cold day. "I'm
sorry?" he said.

"Don't play stupid." The Pirate coach pointed a finger at
Jack. "Your batter is female."

The umpire, every kid on the field, even the fans in the
bleachers followed the finger. They all stared at Jack while

Jack simply stood by, her bat on her shoulder, staring out at center field.

"That so, batter?" Farley asked. Slowly, she turned to face him. "You a girl under those flannels?"

She met all stares, patiently turning the bat in her grip. "Technically," she said, and laughter tumbled from the bleachers.

Farley made a show of rubbing the back of his neck. "Be damned," he said.

The umpire turned on him, and Tex recognized the pinched, crimson face of Bill Fogarty, the same ump who'd kicked him off the mound after he threw a slider into a kid's knee. "You expect me to believe," Fogarty said, "that you weren't aware of your own player's—" He glanced toward the bleachers and turned a deeper shade of red. "You didn't know she was a girl?"

Farley heaved a sigh and gave up. "Course I knew, Bill. So what?"

"So you just forfeited," the Pirate coach answered. "That's what."

Farley's eyes darkened, his jaw muscles twitched, and for the first time that day Tex was glad to be on his side. Farley stepped past Fogarty as if to get a better look at the other coach. "Let me get this straight, Lawrence." A few Twins tittered, but grew quickly sober at Farley's glance. "Let me get this straight. You're pulling out because one biddy girl stepped up to the plate? She too much for your boys to handle?" He turned to address the Pirate infield. "That so, boys? You scared of her?"

"We ain't scared of her or you."

Farley gave Silver Tooth a friendly smile, all the menace gone from his face. "That's just fine, son. That's what I thought. You and the other boys didn't work your butts off all summer just to walk away without proving yourselves."

Listening to him, Tex was reminded of his father, and sought him out. He was still at first base, holding his post. He stood at ease, one elbow cupped in the opposite hand, lightly tapping fingers on lips that wanted very badly, Tex could tell, to smile. But how could that be? How could you know the worst about Farley and still want to smile at what he did best?

Lawrence seemed to be rifling his brain for something to say. "That's not the point and you know it," he said at last.

"What is the point?" Farley demanded.

"Rules!"

"Yeah, well, my guys took a vote and decided the rules were wrong."

"Oh, they *voted*. Why didn't you say so? I'm sure the regional director will be glad to know it."

"You go tell him, Larry. In the meantime, my guys intend to show your guys how to play the game of baseball."

"In your dreams, fatso," Silver Tooth said.

"Attaboy!" said Farley.

Lawrence appealed to Fogarty. "You just gonna stand there, Bill?" Fogarty removed his umpire's cap to scratch a skull as glossy and hairless as a batting helmet. He turned to the bleachers and was met by a grand jury of wives and mothers, the verdict shining out of their eyes like high-beams. He replaced his cap with an angry twist and said, "I call balls and strikes. You boys wanna debate social issues, do it someplace else. This here's a ballpark, so we might as well play ball."

Lawrence opened his mouth, but closed it when Silver Tooth slugged his mitt and lit out for left field.

Everyone returned to where he'd been before, Farley to the third-base coach's box, the Pirate coach to his bench, players to their positions. Jack resumed her stance, and Silver Tooth readied himself in left field, looking pretty cocky, Tex thought, for a kid who'd just stopped a ball game to rat out a girl. The kid was playing deep, as if Dunsmore were at the plate, but when he realized he was alone out there, he spit once and came back in, way in, to complete a shallow fence of boys, a rim of low expectations.

The pitcher nodded to his catcher, wound up, and sent his fastball.

It couldn't have been possible, but in that suspended instant Tex thought he saw Jack smile. She stepped into the pitch and brought the bat around in an arc that hardly seemed to notice the impact, a modest *crack* that nonetheless sent the ball sailing over the center fielder's head. Silver Tooth sped for the fence, grappled briefly with his teammate, stood with the ball, and heaved it in.

Zimmerman scored, and Jack rounded second and headed for third. Farley took a look at the throw and pushed out his hands for her to hold up. She ran by him and headed for home. The shortstop snagged the ball on the hop, turned, and sent it on as Jack flung herself down the baseline, helmet bobbing, sneakers churning, hands out like Superman, flying now, as airborne as the ball, and the both of them converging on home plate, where all three physical forces, ball, catcher, and runner, collided with a thunderclap of gear and bones.

For a moment only the dust moved, settling slowly over the wreckage of arms and legs. Finally, hovering like a medic, Bill Fogarty made an X of his arms and threw them decisively apart.

Safe.

Twins stormed the infield to help her up. Scratched and bleeding, she got a hand even from Dunsmore. Tex rushed out with his teammates, but when Farley arrived, eager to reprimand her with a bear hug, he turned around and walked back to the bench.

Jack joined him there as the game resumed.

"You're insane," he informed her.

She touched her lip, stared at the smear of blood on her fingertip. "I know."

Caroline made a cautious, motherly approach, but Jack gave her the thumbs-up and she returned to the bleachers, shaking her head.

"But I couldn't stop, Tex. Once I got going I knew I had to go all the way, you know?"

"Yeah," he said dismally. "I know."

The Twins were inspired, and he watched in a daze as they pounded the ball and ran hard and stole bases. By the end of the inning they were down by only two runs, and Tex hauled himself from the bench knowing he'd have to throw more artfully than ever.

Four fingers, like a pitchfork, stabbed him in the chest.

"Not so fast, Lefty." Tex had time to wonder which hand

these fingers belonged to, the one that crawled up Jack's leg or the other one, before noticing that Farley wasn't looking at him, but beyond him, at the bench. He removed his fingers from Tex's chest and jerked a thumb toward the diamond. "Let's go, slugger," he said. "Hustle out."

Jack shook her head.

Farley took a step toward her. "What do you mean?"

She shrugged. "I mean I want to sit here, if it's all right with you."

"Of course it's not all right with me. You're a player, now, darlin'. You gotta get out there with the rest of them."

Jack considered the rest of them, shook her head again. "That's just it. I appreciate the chance to play and all, but it ain't fair. Those boys been playing all season. Tex and the others, Frog and Wrig and Big D. It's their pennant."

Farley pointed across the infield. "Is it Larry? Trust me, that weenie ain't gonna say a word."

"It's not him. I got my hit. That was enough, and if you don't mind, Dad, I think I'll just buff the pine here a spell." To show she meant business, she took off a sneaker and began shaking out the dirt.

Farley sighed. "Okay, darlin'. It's your call. Tex, keep her company. You've pitched a good game."

It took a moment for these words to reach him, but when they did they landed like slaps. "You're taking me out?"

Farley squeezed his shoulder, making him wince. "Time for a fresh arm out there."

"I got fifty good throws left, Farley. I swear." He looked around at Jack, at his teammates, searching for an ally, but they all lowered their heads or turned away, and Tex knew how Lucinda Barnes felt in that courtroom, her eyes like wild birds seeking a place to land. He felt the sting of tears and realized, suddenly, that he was telling the truth—that he wanted to pitch to win. Without fully understanding why, he no longer wanted to hurt Farley. He only wanted to help the Twins.

"Please, Coach," he begged. "I can pitch to these bums. I can put 'em away. Please."

Farley looked for a moment as if he might actually change his mind. But then his mind slammed shut, and he told Rummelhart to take the mound, leaving Tex to find his bleary, stunned way to the bench.

"Don't sweat it, Tex," Jack said. "Sometimes it's hard to see what's best for the team. But you gotta sacrifice."

He stared at the blood on her lip and knew that all the hatred he'd been feeling for Farley was totally useless. Farley hadn't done a thing to him personally, he'd done it to Jack. And Tex just happened to see it. And every minute he spent pretending he hadn't was more unbearable than any confession or loss of friendship could ever be.

"Screw that," he said.

"What?"

"Screw the game."

"What's your problem?"

"You know what my problem is."

She glanced up in alarm, but Farley was hanging on to the backstop, too intent on his own nonstop chatter to hear anything else. Yet she said to Tex in a menacing whisper, "Don't start up with that again. Not here."

"We gotta tell, Jack. We gotta do something no matter what."

She began a strange, mechanical shaking of her head, the way Willa May would refuse a spoonful of baked beans, and Tex had to look away.

What he wanted more than anything, he decided, was a bus. The kind you saw on the highway with the tinted windows way up in the air and the destination plastered all over it as if the people inside wanted the whole world to know they were headed to OMAHA, or CLEVELAND. Tex's bus would pull up right here, right now, and its destination would be ANYPLACE BUT HERE.

He was up in that bus, looking out through dark windows, when his eyes fell on the bleachers and the tint suddenly lifted and a thought sizzled through him like voltage.

Yet he stopped himself from blurting it right out. Forced himself to wait. Go slow. Think like a lawyer.

Presently he produced a sigh and turned back to the bleachers. "She's growing up fast, huh," he observed, very much out of the blue.

Jack followed his gaze. Willa May had discovered the pleasures of stomping in the loose dirt in front of the bleachers. "Gonna need a room of her own, pretty soon," Tex said. "Don't you think?"

Jack stared at the girl for a long time, then returned her attention to the game. She crossed her arms tightly. "He ain't gonna be this way forever, Tex. He's just going through a hard time right now. My mom dying and all."

Tex forced himself to speak calmly, reasonably, as his father would. "I don't think so, Jack. I don't think he's ever gonna change till he *has* to. Till somebody *makes* him." She didn't argue, and he rushed ahead. "My dad says there's ways nobody ever has to know a thing, Jack. He says—"

Her eyes were on him like hornets. "You *did* tell him! I knew it—"

"No I didn't—"

"—you squealed like a pig!"

"Will ya shut up? I didn't tell him. I just stopped by his office, and the next thing I know he's talking like he already knows all about it, like he was just sitting there, waiting for me."

Her jaw twitched in a familiar, muscular way, reminding Tex that she was Farley's kid, his natural daughter. Farley was in her blood the way Jacob was in his.

"I swear, Jack," he said. "All I said was I couldn't tell him anything 'cause I promised I wouldn't. Then he started telling me all this stuff about how you—I mean, *a kid*, and a kid's dad, could get help without anybody knowing anything. He said even if there was a trial or something, it'd be totally closed to the public."

Her face paled and she turned away. "Tex, you are so ignorant it's not even funny. You saw what happened to that waitress. There ain't a single person at this ballpark doesn't know all about it, and if you think it'd be any different if her trial had been *closed to the public*, then you think even worse than you pitch."

He stared at the dirt between his cleats with a strange buzzing in his ears like many bees. He couldn't take it. He got up and walked away.

He didn't get far before his father fell in step beside him. "What's the verdict, son?"

"She's stubborn as a damn rock. But I just don't care anymore." He stopped and faced him. "Dad, I saw him. I—"

Jacob raised a hand. "It's not important right now how you know, Tex." He put a hand on his shoulder and kept it there while the boy took several deep breaths. When Tex was calm again, Jacob smiled and put his hands in his pockets. "Thirsty? We've got some time before the next inning."

Tex nodded, and they continued on to the concession stand.

Jack was at the bleachers when they returned, standing next to Caroline, Willa May squirming in her dirty, scratched-up arms. "You tell him?" she asked Tex.

"Tell him what?" Caroline asked.

Tex nodded.

"Figured." Jack pressed her face to Willa May's curls, then glanced at Caroline. "It's okay, Caroline. I mean, I'm fine and all. But I can't tell you. I can't say it." She looked around the park, a little wildly. "I gotta go sit down. On the bench." She handed Willa May to Caroline and, listing strangely, walked away.

Tex just stood there, cold to the bone, until Jack stopped and turned to face him.

"Well," she said. "You comin' or what?"

22

The Twins had come in to bat but nobody seemed much interested in sitting; if they weren't batting or on deck or on base, Tex's teammates were clinging like monkeys to cyclone fencing, and so he and Jack had the entire bench to themselves. From across a considerable span of it he heard her clap for a hit and forced himself to clap as well, just to have something to do with his hands. He thought to look around for his parents, to see where they'd wandered off to, but then thought better of it. He didn't want to see his mother's face the moment his father told her about Farley.

And so Tex just sat there, pretending to watch the game, trying to breathe. If only Jack would look at him, or say his name, then maybe he could relax a little. Maybe the jagged piece of stone in his throat would loosen and drop.

In a moment he felt fingertips to the back of his neck, but when he turned, full of hope, it was his mother. She sat down, filling the space between him and Jack, her back to the game, and stared at Tex for so long and with such intense blue sobriety that dread grabbed his heart. Jack was right, he thought: you couldn't tell a mother and expect anything but a slap in the face.

"What?" he demanded.

In a whisper she said, "Baby," and it was all he could do, suddenly, not to throw himself into her arms. "Ma," he said. "I'm sorry!"

"Tex." She touched his face, smiling as sadly as he'd ever seen her smile. "I have so much to say and no time, just now, to say it. Do you understand?" Her glance drifted across the infield, to Farley, it seemed, at third base. He watched degrees of distress flash across her eyes, injury and dismay and anger, and a confusion he couldn't even bear to see. He looked away, horrified by what he'd done, the landslide of pain his mouth had set in motion.

Caroline gave The Hand a squeeze. "We'll talk later, all right? At your father's."

He nodded, not understanding, and she turned to Jack.

"Come with me, baby," was all she said.

Jack leaned for a look at him, but Tex only hung his head, ashamed of his emotions. When he finally did look up, they had collected Willa May and were well on their way to the parking lot. As he watched, wondering what they could possibly be thinking, or saying, his mother held out her hand, and Jack, to Tex's amazement, took it.

"Hey, Davy. Hey, Donleavy."

Tex blinked his eyes into focus and found Dunsmore before him, staring through cyclone fencing.

"What," he said.

"Looks like I gotta save your ass *again*."

It was the bottom of the sixth and the Twins were down by three with two outs, the bases loaded. Standing near third, Farley pawed absently at his chest, maybe touching the plastic cigar cylinder in his pocket, maybe wiping sweat from his palms.

"Let's go, batter," the umpire called. Dunsmore continued to stare at Tex as if he still wanted to knock the crap out of him—not because he had it coming, Tex knew, but because it was what the two boys were to each other and anything else might send the world fouling off into oblivion.

He looked beyond Dunsmore, to first base, where his father stood by, stroking his chin. Tex stared at him hard and hoped he'd see how little he cared, how absurd the entire game, baseball itself, had become in his mind.

Jacob stopped stroking his chin and gave him a nod.

Tex turned back to Dunsmore. "Shove it," he said.

Dunsmore grinned and went to the plate. He swung at the first pitch, and the crack of the bat released a cry from the fans that seemed to follow, like a choir's voice, the scales of the ball as it climbed up and up, until finally the ball was gone and the cry was on its own and entire families rushed from the bleachers and lined up behind the plate to welcome Dunsmore home.

Tex ducked behind the bleachers and made for the water fountain. He took what was probably the longest drink of his life, and by the time he returned, Farley had lit his cigar and his teammates were joining their parents for the drive to Shakey's Pizza. No one seemed to be looking for him, not even his father, who sat alone on the lowest bench of the empty bleachers. Farley shared a few last grins with Bill Fogarty, then bagged up the team's gear and carried it over to Jacob. He tossed the duffel to the ground as if he'd just lugged it home from the war.

"Where's Caroline?" he boomed. "Where's my beautiful girls!"

Jacob stood up. "They've gone on. In my car."

"Why'd they do that?" Farley glanced around, but saw only Tex. "There you are! Where you been hiding, son? Get on over here and let me congratulate you."

Jacob caught Tex's eye with a steady glance meant, Tex supposed, to reassure him. He began a slow shuffle toward the men.

"The girls have gone on," Jacob told Farley, "but not to the restaurant." He reached out and, with some firmness, tugged Tex by the jersey, drawing him closer. "I doubt we'll be going, either."

Farley squinted as if the sun were in his eyes. He tapped ash into a nearby trash can. "What's going on, Jacob?"

"Can we sit a minute?" Jacob indicated the bleachers, and Farley, after a moment's hesitation, complied with a slap to his knees. Jacob sat down and signaled Tex to take the seat by his side. Tex did, glad to get off legs that felt like sponges, but wary of his father's behavior, or lack of it—that same maddening calm he carried into a courtroom, that deadly politeness he used to turn waitresses into lying nymphos right before your eyes. It was some trick when judges and bailiffs were around to appreciate it, but Tex thought of Ray Stucky, and the quickness of Farley's fist, and hoped his father would not attempt it here.

"Well, Counselor," Farley said. He savored his Cuban cigar with great amusement. "You've gotten us all together here. What's on your mind?"

Jacob looked out over the diamond. Far beyond the fence, in the vicinity of Dunsmore's homer, a dog was running through soybeans, leaping to see where it was going, its yellow head like a tennis ball bouncing along a vast green court. Tex was shocked by the height and density of the crop; he remembered when the plants had been just shoots in the soil, barely visible, but he didn't remember anything in between.

"Laws," Jacob said at last. "Laws are on my mind."

"Laws," Farley said, trying the word out. He leaned forward for a look at Tex, as if he might explain. Tex looked away.

Jacob brushed something from his knee. "I was thinking, in particular, that the laws in Iowa are strange."

Farley glanced at his watch. "How so?"

"Well, for instance, the federal government has recently passed an act that is extremely detailed in terms of the legal definition of child abuse."

Farley bit the wet end of his cigar, poker-faced.

"Yet in Iowa," Jacob went on, "there is still no specific statute for the prosecution of a perpetrator of child abuse. We have civil codes for removing the child from an abusive environment, but no criminal laws for punishing or reforming the abuser."

"That is strange," Farley said.

"Yes," Jacob agreed. "Strange enough for our courts to compensate—overcompensate, some would say—in dealing with reports of child abuse. Especially any reports involving sexual activity."

Farley shook his head. He grunted appreciatively, and rose abruptly from the bleacher. "That's damned interesting, Jacob. God damned if it ain't. But now how's about telling me where I can find my family, and we can resume this little chat at a later date?" Tex could hear the breath in Farley's nostrils. He seemed to have gained fifty pounds in the shoulders and arms.

Jacob watched him, unmoved. "Ten minutes, Farley. If you'll give me ten minutes, I think you'll be glad you did."

"I think I'd be gladder if you said whatever you have to say to me in private, for Chrissake, and not in front of this boy."

Tex had to agree with him there.

"I would, believe me," Jacob said. "But he happens to know it all already."

Farley stared at Tex, his eyes and cigar smoldering, three points in a hot triangle. He stared for some time, then slowly resumed his seat.

A pair of ducks flew by, their wings beating the air with unnatural volume. At last Farley took the bait.

"What is it, exactly, he thinks he knows?"

Tex grabbed aluminum with both hands: the bleachers were tilting like a ride at the carnival.

"More than he cares to," Jacob said. "Some time ago, on nothing more than a gut feeling, really, I asked him a favor. I asked him to keep his eyes open. I asked him to look out for Jack." He looked at Tex, but Tex wouldn't look back, had locked his eyes on the partial imprint of somebody's rubber cleats, a pair of holes punched into dirt like empty eye sockets.

216

"I wish I could take that request back, now," his father continued, his voice less sturdy. "I wish I'd come to you directly, man to man, and left him out of it." He fell silent and even seemed to slouch a little, maybe for the first time in his life, it crossed Tex's mind. But when he spoke again, his voice was sure. "But I didn't, and now he's become a factor."

"A factor."

"Yes."

"A factor in what?"

"In this."

Farley stared at him, a man with no time for games. "And this is what, Jacob? A bad joke?"

"I wish it were, Farley. I truly do. But the fact is I've seen lives torn apart, reputations demolished, children taken from their parents and forced to testify against them in court—all on less evidence of impropriety than exists here."

Tex could not believe his ears. *Reputations? Court?* "What happened to no one ever hearing a word about it?" he wanted to howl. Had his father lied to get him to say what he knew?

"Excuse me, Counselor," Farley said, interrupting his panic. "But unless I'm badly misunderstanding something here, you're threatening me with some kind of—"

"No one's threatening you."

"Call it what you want, you're threatening me with some kind of big legal stink based on some half-baked ideas this boy may have gotten from my daughter? Don't you think he's got more sense than that? Don't you think he's got more dignity?"

Tex's response was quick, if mumbled. "Lot you know about dignity."

"What did you say?"

217

"It won't be a question of dignity," Jacob said, "if we have to deal with this in court. Given the circumstances, Tex would most likely be *required* to testify. He and Jack both."

"And you'd have no problem with that, I suppose? Dragging your own kid into court?"

Jacob adjusted his glasses. "There are worse things a father can do."

It seemed like a good time for them all to turn and watch the dog in the soybean field. Its head was just a yellow dot, now, appearing less and less frequently as it moved toward a distant farmhouse. Each time the yellow dot went down, Tex held his breath until it popped back up again.

"And there it is," Jacob said. "I just wanted to let you know what might happen if we have to deal with this in civil court." He leaned forward a little, as if he were thinking about getting up and going home. Tex leaned forward, too.

"Which is to say nothing of criminal court," Jacob said. Going nowhere.

"Criminal court? Hold on, now." Farley gave the time-out signal. "Didn't you start out this whole lecture saying how *strange* it was that Iowa has no, what's the word . . ."

"Statute for child abuse? That's right. Which is why the county attorney might, at the very least, try to put you in jail on the charge of wanton neglect of children. He might be inclined to prosecute for lascivious acts with children. Or incest."

Tex's entire body chilled at the word, as if falling through ice—all but The Hand, that hated, ugly thing at the end of his arm, burning with shame.

218

His father paused, allowing Farley the chance to interject a fresh cloud of Cuban smoke.

"Conceivably," Jacob continued, "you could stand trial for rape."

Farley removed what was left of his cigar, attempted to whistle, stuck it back in. "It's beginning to sound like you wouldn't be my first choice for a lawyer, Jacob."

"Nobody's been charged with anything, Farley. Nobody has to be. Nobody has to go to court, and nobody but the three of us here, Jack and Caroline, and a few discreet professionals—"

Farley's head jerked around. "Caroline?"

The two men stared at each other.

"She is," Jacob said, "concerned."

"Is that right." Farley looked as though he were trying to crush rocks with his molars. "Well, bless her soul."

Tex watched him and felt a fresh wave of hatred on his mother's behalf—on behalf of her left ear, to be exact, into which Farley had once sung a corny song.

"She only wants what's best for Jack," Jacob said. "That's all any of us want."

Farley shifted his gaze, and Tex had to look away. "You think this is what's best for her, Tex? You think this is what she wants?"

"I know what she doesn't want," he said to his cleats.

"You seem to know a hell of a lot, all of a sudden. What's gotten into you, son?"

Tex looked up at the word *son* and didn't look away. "Facts," he said.

Farley's eyes bored into him. "What are the facts, Tex?"

Jacob raised a hand. "He is not obliged—"

"I'm talking to Tex," Farley said, his eyes on the boy.

"You know what they are," Tex said.

"You're damn right I do. The fact is you've gotten ahold of some pretty screwy ideas and are about to make a big, big mistake."

Tex's eyes burned, his chest heaved, and he said in a wild rush, "I don't care! If it keeps you out of her room, if it keeps you from—"

Farley was on his feet. He hovered over Jacob and Tex as if he meant to stop the whole thing right there.

Jacob stood up. "Farley—"

"Who do you think you are? The two of you, talking to me like this?" A vein squirmed under the skin of his temple like a worm cut in half.

"Let's all calm down a minute—"

"You want me to calm down? I tell you what—" He spun, looking for something—for the duffel—and Tex jumped to his feet.

"You *touch* her!" he cried. "You touch her at night and you make me sick!"

Farley whipped around, forgetting the duffel, his face a mask of red. He took a step forward, but Tex held his ground—or appeared to. In fact he couldn't have moved if he wanted to, but it worked, for Farley came no farther. The rage drained from his face and a look of deep confusion, of bafflement came over him. "You're gonna believe what she told you? Just like that?"

"No," Tex said. "I'm gonna believe what I saw."

"What you saw . . ." He dragged a hand over his face, suddenly exhausted. "You didn't see a thing, Tex."

"I shouldn't have, but I did. And if you don't believe me, then ask her. Ask Jack if I was there. Ask your best girl. Your sweetest sweetheart. Your best little—" He gulped back a sob and sat down hard, and Farley took a strange, stumbling backward step. He steadied himself against the trash can.

Jacob found his voice again. "None of this *has* to happen, Farley. That's why I wanted to talk to you first."

Farley stared fixedly at the space between Jacob and Tex.

"Farley?" Jacob said. "Farley."

Farley shut his eyes. Gave his head a slight shake. "What."

"I believe I can convince Mr. Gray, the county attorney, to allow you to be considered for a criminal diversion program."

Farley opened his eyes, but didn't seem able to focus. "A what?"

"It's a kind of contract. You admit to what you've done, undergo treatment for it, and agree to any other provisions the court requires. Then, once you've completed the program, your record will be expunged."

"Hey," he said weakly. "Sounds like a snap."

"Take the contract, Farley, and you'll not only avoid an open court hearing but you'll keep these kids from having to testify. You'll keep your family together. And you'll get to keep coaching."

Farley stared at what was left of his cigar. "You've called me a lot of things today, Jacob, but that's the first time you've called me stupid."

Jacob just stared at him, not getting it.

"I'm never coaching again, and you know it. Not in this

221

county, probably not in this state. The minute you go to the law or the social witch-hunters or whoever, you might as well take out a full-page ad in the *Observer*: 'Little Leaguers, Beware!' Hell, we might as well go to Shakey's. I just won my last game."

Tex expected his father to disagree, but he only shrugged and said, "You can't help what people will think, Farley."

Farley nodded and looked away, toward the outfield fence. Tex looked beyond, for the dog, but it was gone.

"How long do I have to decide?" Farley asked.

"Monday morning."

He sucked on the stub of his cigar, scowled at it, then tossed it in the trash can. He nodded again, kept nodding until, at some point Tex didn't notice, nodding became shaking. "Had to happen here, didn't it? Had to happen at the ballpark."

Then he bent for the duffel, slung it over his shoulder, and set a steady, straightforward course for the parking lot, as if he truly meant to join his team for pizza.

Tex watched him go, his heart pounding in his throat. "What's that supposed to mean?"

Jacob shook his head as if he had no idea, but answered anyway. "I guess it means he wishes we'd done this anyplace but here."

Anyplace But Here, Tex thought grimly, remembering his bus. He watched Farley walk away and knew they couldn't have done it anywhere else, that this was the one place the three of them had ever had in common. He watched him walk away and thought of the Spaldings huddled together down in

222

that duffel, scuffed green and brown, his own fingerprints all over them, and knew he'd never see them again. They were simply gone, like Linda. Farley carried them away along with the bats and the helmets and all the other gear of summer. He carried dirt and grass, Tex thought, the chatter of teammates, the shade of a cap, the smell of a mitt, the pain of throwing strikes.

And he carried Jack.

23

"Let's go, son," Jacob said after some minutes. Tex turned to scan the parking lot and saw nothing there now but a wisp of gravel dust, the ghost of the last vehicle to leave, which had been Farley's minibus.

"How?" he said, and his father raised one dusty wing tip. "With these." He stood, took one clownish step, then another, until Tex shook his head and got to his feet. His legs were still shaky, but they came back to him when he spotted something on the ground, a piece of gear Farley had missed, lying in the dirt beneath the Twins' bench. He jogged over to collect it, then jogged back to his father, and they began to walk.

His father did it well, Tex learned. They only stopped once, and only then because Manny had not yet locked up and they were thirsty. For once, the barber did not seem personally offended that people had come into his shop for anything less than a haircut, but instead joked with Jacob and even gave Tex two dimes for the cooler.

Later, coming upon the Route 61 Diner, once a tempting sight, Jacob and Tex agreed there was no need to stop, as they'd just finished their Cokes. They walked on and wore out the day's warmth, and the sun's loft, and much of the bite, Tex figured, from his rubber cleats. By the time they reached their street they were both limping slightly but doing so, Tex thought, with some pride, as if their journey had been completed against odds that nobody, save the two of them, would ever fully understand.

Then they reached the driveway, and Tex was jolted out of such thoughts. Sitting there, the Thunderbird was the prelude to the scene his father had tried, as offhandedly as possible, to prepare him for, which was nothing more than walking in and seeing his mother, and Jack, in his own house. He might've faced one at a time and been all right, he thought, but he didn't like his chances for seeing both of them together and not completely falling to pieces.

He was, therefore, considering the various ways he could get to his room undetected—he knew several—when he caught a glimpse of blue beyond the corner of the house, and Jack came into view. Or rather, hopped into view, engaged, it seemed, in some solo version of backyard hopscotch.

"There's Jack," Tex said.

"Yes," said Jacob. They watched her for a moment, hopping away with all the single-mindedness of Willa May stomping in dirt, until Tex began to wonder if she hadn't gone a little bit crazy. He felt a hand on his shoulder, and when Jacob spoke, the words buzzed in his bones like the hum of a bat. "I hope you understand, Tex. Those things I said about families, about what I've seen happen. I'm not saying it *will*. I was only trying—"

"I know, Dad," Tex said. And he did. He'd figured it out on the long walk home. In his own maddening, long-winded way, his father had presented yet another Hobson's choice: Farley could take the contract, try to get help for himself and his daughter, or he could risk losing her altogether, even going to jail. As he and his father walked, Tex had heard again Farley's drunken voice, telling Jack she was all he had, how he'd be lost without her. And he'd understood for the first time what a Hobson's choice really was. It was no choice at all. Unless he was crazy, unless there was absolutely no truth to the man he'd been to Tex all summer long, Farley would have to choose the contract. He'd *have* to. For her. For Jack.

"Okay," Jacob said, giving his shoulder a final squeeze. "I'm going inside."

"Okay."

The door banged shut and Jack stopped jumping. Saw Tex standing there. Smiled.

She waved him over.

"Have you felt this grass?" she asked, jumping again.

"Uh, yeah," he said, keeping an eye on her.

"Can you imagine a whole outfield of this grass? That must be what it's like in the majors. Watch." She pulled a ball from her mitt and flung it at the ground. It sprang back up, knee-high, into her mitt.

Tex took a small, tentative hop. It *was* pretty springy.

She cocked her head at him.

"What?" he said.

"Whaddaya hiding?"

"Oh." He pulled his mitt out from behind his back. Opened it up.

She looked, and smiled. "My cap."

"It was at the park."

"I forgot I threw it in the duffel."

"Yeah," he said. "It must've fallen out."

She tossed off the blue Twins cap, replaced it with red. "So," she said, tugging on the bill.

"So what?"

"So don't you have something to tell me?"

His heart felt like that ball—bounced off the ground, but with no mitt to catch it. He did not want to go back to those bleachers. Did not want to remember the things his father said. Did not want to remember the look on Farley's face.

Definitely did not want to tell Jack any of it.

Yet he'd have to, he knew; he'd broken his promise, and he owed her, and she had a right to know, and—

"The game, Tex?" she said.

"The game . . . ?"

"Did we win?"

The game! Relief gushed into his chest. His heart calmed down, and he was able, to his surprise, to describe the final inning with a drama he hadn't felt at the time—how the Twins fought off full counts, found the gaps, and loaded up the bases. How Dunsmore brought them all home with a single swing. Jack listened patiently, and when Tex was done she gave a nod, as if she'd guessed as much.

He didn't know what to say after that, and they both spent some time digging their toes into the grass.

"Thanks, Tex," she said at last.

"For what?"

His question, or his tone, seemed to catch her off guard—but then she tapped a finger on the red bill. "For this."

"Oh," he said. "Sure." But he didn't much like being thanked, he discovered. He clenched his mitt shut and stared at it, and in a rush his mind went flying back in time, to the day he met her, to the Archibald, their bare feet in cool water, both their hands inside her mitt, her fingers guiding his into place so that he might wear, for the first time in his life, a baseball glove. So that he might play the game, open a can of Coke, shake a teammate's hand. She'd given him his right hand back, and Farley had shown him what he could do with it. Together they'd not only made him a ballplayer, they'd made him whole. And this was how he'd repaid them.

He wanted to run back across the county, suddenly. He wanted to find Farley and tell him he didn't mean it, that they could all forget everything and go on.

But it was too late. Dusk was purpling the sky, his mother and father and Willa May were up on the porch, watching, and Jack was standing in his own backyard, ready to throw the ball.

FIC
JOH

Johnston, Tim.

Never so green

DATE DUE	BORROWER'S NAME	ROOM NO.

FIC
JOH

Johnston, Tim.

Never so green